**BEWARE!!
DO NOT READ THIS
BOOK FROM
BEGINNING TO END!**

DISCARDED

Pee-yew! What *stinks*?

Your new house is right next to Stinkeye Swamp. There's only one good thing about it: A legend says there's treasure hidden nearby. Maybe in the swamp. Or maybe even in your basement.

You want that treasure! But to find it, you'll have to deal with some bad stuff. Like dark tunnels. Man-traps. Flesh-eating fish. And very angry ghosts.

Oh, and one other thing. The legend also says that the treasure is cursed. . . .

This scary adventure is all about you. You decide what will happen — and how terrifying the scares will be!

Start on PAGE 1. Then follow the instructions at the bottom of each page. You make the choices. If you choose well, you'll survive. You may even end up rich! But if you make the wrong choice . . . BEWARE!

SO TAKE A DEEP BREATH. CROSS YOUR FINGERS. AND TURN TO PAGE 1 TO *GIVE YOURSELF GOOSEBUMPS!*

READER BEWARE —
YOU CHOOSE THE SCARE!

Look for more
GIVE YOURSELF GOOSEBUMPS adventures
from R.L. STINE

R.L. STINE

GIVE YOURSELF

Goosebumps®

LOST IN STINKEYE SWAMP

AN
APPLE
PAPERBACK

SCHOLASTIC INC.
New York Toronto London Auckland Sydney

A PARACHUTE PRESS BOOK

No part of this publication may be reproduced in whole or in part, or stored in a retrieval system, or transmitted in any form or by any means, electronic, mechanical, photocopying, recording, or otherwise, without written permission of the publisher. For information regarding permission, write to Scholastic Inc., 555 Broadway, New York, NY 10012.

ISBN 0-590-39775-3

12 11 10 9 8 7 6 5 4 3 2   7 8 9/9 0 1 2/0

Printed in the U.S.A.   40

First Scholastic printing, December 1997

"Swamp House?" you shriek. You gaze out the car window at the words painted on the mailbox. "You didn't tell me our new house is called *Swamp House!*"

Your dad steers the station wagon down the long, bumpy driveway. "You'll love it," he assures you.

Then you get a look at the house. It's a dump! It's huge, run-down, and ancient looking. The white paint is dirty and peeling. Half the shutters are hanging by one hinge.

"It's a fixer-upper," your dad says as he parks the car.

More like a knocker-downer, you think.

You get out of the car and take a deep breath. Yuck! What smells so gross? You gaze around and see that the house sits next to a big, ugly swamp.

"That's Stinkeye Swamp," your dad explains as you all start unpacking the car. "Fifty square miles of wilderness, right in our backyard. Isn't it great?"

"Whoopee," you mutter.

"The swamp is supposed to be haunted," your mom adds. "And they say there's buried treasure around here. There's even a legend about 'Annabelle's Curse.'" She shivers. "Oooooh!"

Turn to PAGE 2.

"Mom," you groan. You know she's faking.

She punches you playfully on the shoulder. "What a grouch," she teases. "You know you *love* creepy stuff like ghosts and legends."

You'd never admit it, but your mom is right. The stuff about the treasure and the legend sound cool. The ghost part is lame, though.

"Welcome to Stinkeye Swamp," a voice calls.

You drop the carton you're holding and turn around. A boy about your age approaches. He has a pale face and long black hair.

"I'm Zeke," he tells you. He gazes past you at the house. "So someone finally bought Swamp House."

You sigh. "My parents," you mutter. "The Fixer-Uppers."

Zeke laughs. "Well, there's plenty of fixing up to do here. But that could be cool," he adds. "It will keep your parents out of your hair."

For the first time since you heard about moving, you smile. "Hey — you've got a point," you say. A broad grin spreads across your face.

You like the way this kid thinks!

Turn to PAGE 3.

You and Zeke end up being great friends. He doesn't go to your school, but you hang out together every afternoon. Zeke's biggest drawback? He's totally obsessed with Annabelle's Curse and finding the treasure.

"Come on, what have we got to lose?" Zeke urges one afternoon for the millionth time.

You roll your eyes. "I'm tired of looking for treasure!" you tell him. "That's all you ever want to do. We've searched the whole house a hundred times already."

It's Friday after school. Your parents are at work. You and Zeke are playing catch in the weed-infested backyard.

"Come on!" Zeke replies. "Even if there's no treasure, we might find something down there."

"Down there" is the basement of Swamp House. You haven't searched there yet — because the basement *stinks*. It smells just like Stinkeye Swamp.

With a shrug, you follow him. Who knows? Maybe you'll dig up some old comic books. Those might be worth something.

Descend to PAGE 4.

4

You step from the hot sun into the damp, cold basement. It's even worse than you expected. Old rotted chairs are stacked to the ceiling, along with crumbling papers, moldy trunks, piles of rags, rusty tin cans, an old sewing machine, and about three hundred cardboard boxes.

"There's nothing here," you complain to Zeke after a few minutes of poking around. You're already bored. And you have a creepy feeling that there might be a large rat or two crawling around behind some of the boxes.

Zeke is on his hands and knees in the dust. "Wait!" he cries, popping up. "Look at this!" He holds out a bright, gleaming tube.

"Cool!" you exclaim. "An old telescope."

In the glaring light of the bare bulb, the brass cylinder shines brightly. Almost as if it's glowing.

"It's something a ship's captain would use," Zeke comments, turning it in his hands. Letters are etched on the sides.

"Hey, let me see," you demand. You take a few steps toward Zeke — and trip over something on the floor.

"Whoa!" you yell.

You're going down!

Trip onto PAGE 5.

You land on top of an old trunk.

"Are you okay?" Zeke asks.

"I tripped over something," you explain. You reach down and pick up an old leather-bound book. It's held shut with a thick strap.

"What's that?" Zeke asks. He walks over.

You study the heavy brown volume. The rich leather of the book's cover shines dully. The pages are bursting out of the binding. One hangs loose. You can see writing in tiny black letters.

"It looks like some kind of diary," you answer.

"Let's open it up and read it!" Zeke exclaims. "Maybe the secret of the Swamp House treasure is in there!"

For the first time, you're as excited as Zeke. You're dying to read the book.

But Zeke is still holding the gleaming telescope. You can't wait to look through that. You could probably see for miles with it.

Which should you do first?

To read the diary, go to PAGE 27.
To peer through the telescope, go to PAGE 25.

You shake your head. "Later," you mouth. With Annabelle staring at you, there's no way you're going to say anything to Zeke.

Still, you can't help worrying that she saw you pick up the large jewel.

The ghost of Annabelle lifts one of her skeletal arms. A beam of light shoots out from her pale white hand.

"We have returned," she cries.

The beam lights up the door to your basement — the very door you and Zeke passed through at the beginning of your adventure.

You can hardly believe it. Annabelle has led you home.

But why?

Find out on PAGE 70.

"What do you mean, you've been lost for twenty years?" you demand.

"Just our luck," Zeke moans. "A sewer worker who's lost in the sewer."

"I may be lost," Ed retorts, "but I know a lot about getting around down here. Come on, I'll show you the work site."

Ed slogs off through the muck on the ground. You and Zeke hesitate for a moment, then hurry to catch up.

A thought occurs to you. "Hey — if you've been down here for twenty years, what have you been eating?"

Ed ignores your question. "This sewer is a very interesting place, what with the treasure and all," he announces.

"Treasure?" you repeat. "So the legend is true!"

"Sure. There's a whole bunch of blue jewels the smugglers lost down here. I'll show you," Ed offers. He takes a few steps.

Then Ed stops and scratches his head. "Problem is, I always get the directions to the treasure mixed up with the way to the sewage recycling plant. That's where I was working when I got lost — the Green Thumb Sewage Treatment and Fertilizer Plant."

"Great!" you murmur. "He's more clueless than we are!"

Try not to get lost on your way to PAGE 55.

"Ouch!" you yelp. "Why did you hit me?"

"Because I didn't want you to fall," Zeke replies.

You aim your flashlight at the ground. You gasp.

The tunnel comes to an abrupt end. A vast black hole stretches in front of you. When you shine the flashlight into it, you can't see anything except darkness.

A very rickety-looking ladder leads into the pit.

"Y-you want to go first?" Zeke sounds nervous.

"Uh — okay." You hand Zeke the flashlight and grab the top of the ladder.

"I wish those smugglers put in an elevator," you joke.

The old ladder buckles with your weight, but it stays attached to the wall. You go down one rung at a time.

"Do you see anything?" Zeke calls out.

"No," you call back as you keep climbing down.

"I'm coming down," Zeke hollers.

"Don't!" you shout. "The ladder won't —"

You were going to say "hold us both." But it's too late. As Zeke puts his weight on the top rung, you feel the ladder sway and twist.

With a sickening snap, it breaks free from the wall!

Land on PAGE 103.

A ball of glowing white light hangs in the air. Then it stretches and shimmers.

And takes the shape of a beautiful teenage girl!

Her long silvery hair floats on the air like tangled vines. Her once-elegant clothing is in rags.

Then she opens her mouth. You can see through to the black emptiness behind her.

"Who dares to enter my world?" she shrieks.

Her right hand stretches out and reaches for you.

"Yikes!" you cry.

You and Zeke jump backwards. Then you turn to run.

Try escaping on PAGE 76.

The force of Annabelle's gaze draws you forward against your will. You stumble over to join Zeke. You both cower on the cavern floor.

Somehow you manage to speak. "Are you the Annabelle of the legend?" you ask. Your voice comes out as a thin squeak.

"I am," the terrible spirit replies. She spreads her ghostly robes as if they were giant wings. "Poor Annabelle — doomed to roam these tunnels forever.

"I was warned to stay away," she continues. "But one night, I crept into these tunnels to get to a ball. Then the curse kept me here forever. Now you must share my fate!"

"Share her fate?" you whisper to Zeke, your teeth chattering. "What does she mean?"

But if Zeke knows the answer, he doesn't tell you before the ghost speaks again.

"Come!" Annabelle commands. "Come and meet your doom!"

She drifts out of the cavern like a fog.

"I'm not going anywhere," you protest. But your feet move on their own! You have no control over your body.

Like a robot, you march after the ghostly girl.

March to PAGE 43.

"What happened?" you demand as you clamber back onto the boat. "Where are the ghosts?"

"I don't know," Zeke replies, looking puzzled. "I thought I was a goner. Then the moon came up."

He points to the full moon above the treetops.

"All the ghosts started screaming and running around. Before I knew it, they were gone."

"Are you ever lucky." You sigh with relief. "Let's look for the treasure."

Zeke nods. "Okay. But before we do that, I want to make sure there aren't any other ghosts around. Let's climb to the roof of the wheelhouse and get a bird's-eye view."

You're eager to find the treasure and get out of there. But Zeke seems anxious to get a look at the ship from the wheelhouse. After what he went through, maybe you should humor him.

Go to the wheelhouse on PAGE 34.
Hunt for treasure on PAGE 59.

"There's something about those goldfish I don't like," you declare.

"Yeah, they look fishy to me too," Zeke agrees.

"Let's try the ledge," you tell him.

Zeke leads the way. The two of you inch onto the ledge around the pool.

The ledge narrows quickly. Soon it's only a few inches wide. You have to lean flat against the rough stone wall.

"Are we almost there?" you ask. You reach out with your toe in the near-darkness. You press against the wall for balance.

"Yup," Zeke replies. "See, I told you this was the right way to — YAAAAIIII!"

The stone wall you're leaning against suddenly collapses. Zeke vanishes through a gaping, jagged hole.

"Zeke!" you shout. You reach out to grab him. But you lose your balance and fall through too.

Drop to PAGE 22.

You follow Carl into the swamp, walking single file along the narrow path. Sometimes the track almost disappears. And sometimes, Carl turns around to warn you of a hidden pool or other danger.

After walking for almost an hour, you come to a large clearing with a sturdy-looking cabin in the middle. There's a little vegetable garden out front and a couple of rough wooden chairs. Carl motions for the two of you to sit down. He hands you each a cup filled with clear, cold water.

"Nice place you have here," you say after a few moments of silence.

"Nice?" Carl replies. "You want to stay?"

"We want to find the treasure," Zeke blurts out.

At the word "treasure," Carl's eyes light up.

"Treasure?" he cries. "Only for those who have the captain's glass!"

"Captain's glass?" you repeat.

"Telescope, some call it," Carl says.

The telescope! You reach down.

It's still in your shirt! You pull it out.

"You mean, like this?" you ask, holding it up.

See your way to PAGE 77.

You step carefully from stone to stone. Zeke is right behind you. Soon you are standing in front of a stone wall.

"We must have goofed," you mutter. "There's no door here." Annoyed, you smack the stones in front of you.

A section of the wall swings back noiselessly.

"We did it!" Zeke cries. "It's the door to the smugglers' tunnel! Let's go!"

You're nervous and excited. The tunnel is dark, and you have no idea where it goes. But now you really believe you could find the treasure.

"We should get some —" You were about to say "supplies," like food, rope, and water. But Zeke brushes past you into the tunnel before you can finish. You grab an old flashlight that's lying on a trunk and rush after him.

"Zeke!" you call, waving the flashlight back and forth. You don't see him. And then you hear something that makes your blood run cold.

The sound of the secret door slamming shut behind you.

Go to PAGE 53.

"Don't let that troublemaker bother you, little brother," Annabelle growls. "I was angry at you for the first fifty years or so. But I got over it. Now let's get out of here!"

The two of them rise toward the ceiling and begin to disappear. Your feet are no longer frozen in place, and you run in circles underneath them. You're so frantic, you even try to jump up and catch them as they drift away.

"Wait!" you shout. "What about me?"

"What about you?" Zeke replies with an evil grin. "You tried to turn my sister against me. You deserve to be left here."

"Don't leave me here!" you beg. "How will I ever get home?"

"Gee, I don't know." He laughs. "Maybe you'll find another doorknob. In about two hundred years!"

He and Annabelle vanish right through the cave ceiling.

When they are gone, everything is pitch-black. Your mind reels with fear. You are trapped deep underground. You have no idea where you are. How will you ever get out?

As the blackness closes in, you realize that Zeke was never really your friend. He just tricked you so you'd lift the curse.

But you'll think of a way to get revenge. After all, you've got plenty of time on your hands!

THE END

"'November 11, 1797,'" you read.

"Wow!" You let out a low whistle. "That's two hundred years ago!"

The edges of the page crumble as you hold it up to keep reading.

"'Dear Diary,

I'll show them! They think they can keep me from dancing with Hubert, but now I have a way of getting to the ball. Today I found the entrance to the old smugglers' tunnel. When they're all asleep I'll be on my way. Won't Hubert be surprised to see me at the ball in my new gown? I can hardly wait.

Annabelle.'

"Annabelle!" you gasp.

"That's the name in the legend," Zeke cries.

You glance back at the page. "Smugglers!" you murmur. "Annabelle says she found a tunnel used by smugglers."

"And where there are smugglers —" Zeke reasons.

"— there's treasure!" you finish. You grin at Zeke. "And we're going to find it!"

Find out more on PAGE 120.

If Billings isn't a ranger, what is he?

An icy fear grips your heart. You think you can guess what Billings is really up to. He wants to steal the telescope and use it to find the treasure hidden in the swamp!

You glance quickly at Billings to make sure he is still asleep.

Yes! He's snoring. You settle down and pore over the map.

The path you're on leads to another river. After it crosses the river, the path divides. One branch goes through something called the Strangler Vines Thicket. The other branch leads back to town — and home!

Then you hear Billings stir in his sleep.

You know you can't trust him anymore. And you can't let him catch you with the map. You roll it up and stuff it back into the case.

Billings turns over. Is he waking up?

Hold your breath and turn to PAGE 81.

You struggle against the plant's tight grip. But it's useless. You see Zeke being lifted up too. You're both hanging upside down. Directly below you, a red flower the size of a small car is slowly opening its petals.

"There's nothing to be sc-sc-scared of," Zeke stammers. "It's just a flower, right?"

You stare into the gaping mouth of the flytrap.

"Yeah," you murmur, shivering. "But how come I see bones down there?"

Just my luck, you think, as you're lowered into the flower. Why couldn't I get caught by a flower that's a vegetarian?

THE END

You stretch out and swim for the log, straining against the current. For a second, you think it's going to sweep right past. But with a final hard kick, you lunge forward. And grasp a small branch jutting from its side.

Zeke grabs hold of the other side. You haul each other up and lie there panting against the wet bark. The log rushes forward in the flood.

As you regain your strength you notice that the light is growing. The log speeds on. Up ahead is the blazing light of day. With a final rush, the water spills out into the open.

You and Zeke find yourselves floating peacefully under a bright blue sky.

You look around. The lake is surrounded by a bright green wall of thick jungle. Trees, bushes, and vines crowd the shore. Insects buzz. You hear the cry of a strange bird.

The two of you paddle the log toward dry ground. You both wade ashore and collapse on the muddy shore.

"Wow, I've never been in this part of Stinkeye Swamp," Zeke says, peering around.

"Stinkeye Swamp?" you repeat. "You mean the swamp that's supposed to be haunted?"

Crawl to PAGE 80.

You carefully take the brittle paper from Zeke and study it.

"It's a word scramble," you announce. "If we unscramble each word, the letters in the circles will spell out a clue, I think."

"The captain told me all the words have something to do with this boat or the river," Zeke replies.

You unscramble the words. You glance down the list and read each letter in the circles. Suddenly you know the answer.

"I've got it!" you cry. "I know where to look for the answer!"

Unscramble the words on the scroll on PAGE 21. Then read the circled letters from top to bottom for a hint about how to break the curse. After that, follow the directions under the scroll.

CKED D E C K

APLDED P a d d l e

ORTP _ _ _ _

EATWR _ _ _ _ _ _

CAINB _ _ _ _ _

RVIRE _ _ _ _ _

NNEGIE _ _ _ _ _ _

EAMTS _ _ _ _ _

LHEWE _ _ _ _ _ _

ATOB _ _ _ _

GFAL _ _ _ _

Take a look at the ship's clock on PAGE 33.
Find the captain's log on PAGE 24.

The two of you crash onto the floor of another tunnel. Luckily, you only fall a few feet.

You stand up. The ground is covered with a thick, oozing muck. You blink several times in the bright light from the bare electric lightbulbs dangling along the ceiling. They seem blinding after the gloom of the cavern.

"Zeke!" you exclaim. "Look at these walls. They're made of cement. And those lightbulbs up there. Where are we now?"

"What's the matter with you kids?" a gruff voice breaks in. "Haven't you ever been in a sewer before?"

You glance up. A man is walking toward you, carrying a shovel and a large wrench over his shoulder. He's wearing dirty orange overalls and high rubber boots. His hair is long and filthy, and his face is almost hidden by a thick black beard.

"You two aren't in the sewer workers' union, are you?" he demands.

Go to PAGE 100.

You recognize the bearded face. It's the stranger you were chasing.

"Caught you, I did!" he shouts gleefully. He shakes his head, and the branches in his hat swish back and forth.

"Who are you?" you shout. "Let us out of here!"

"You can't fool old Carl," the man shouts. "You mean to hurt the swamp!"

"We don't! We're just lost," you plead. "Honest."

The man looks puzzled. He chews his beard thoughtfully. "Can't let you out," he mutters, finally. "Unless you can solve the riddle."

"Riddle?" you repeat hopefully. "What riddle?"

Carl peers down at you.

"Got a ladder, I have," he cries. "And I'll lower it down if you tell me how many rungs it has."

"What?" Zeke complains. "How are we supposed to do that?"

"How? Listen, listen, listen! That's how," Carl declares.

Listen on PAGE 123.

"The captain's log!" you tell Zeke. "Where is it?"

You're not quite used to talking to a ghost, but it's not as frightening as it was at first.

"In his cabin," Zeke replies. "Follow me."

He floats down the main deck of the boat. Then he pushes open a fancy wooden door with a tarnished brass sign on it. The two of you step into the captain's cabin. Zeke hands you a mold-covered leather book.

"Here it is," he announces. "The ship's log. This is where the captain wrote down everything that happened."

Quickly, you flip through the yellow pages, searching for some kind of clue about how to lift the curse.

"How does this old book help me?" Zeke asks.

"Quiet! I'm concentrating," you tell him. "The answer must be here somewhere."

Keep looking on PAGE 129.

You take the telescope from Zeke. The brass cylinder is heavy and cold in your hands. Etched along the side are some words. You read them aloud: "'To see what isn't there.'"

"What is *that* supposed to mean?" You laugh.

Zeke laughs too. He takes the scope back and lifts it to his eye.

Then he stops laughing. He looks as if he's about to drop the scope.

"What?" you demand. "What is it?"

Without a word, Zeke hands you the scope.

You look through it.

On the far wall, outlined in blue light, is a door. But when you take the eyepiece away, the door disappears!

"I can see a door!" you cry as you look through it again. "I bet the treasure is behind it!"

You and Zeke rush to the door. Using the telescope, you spot a hidden latch. You pull it, and the door swings back with a creak. Beyond is a tunnel into blackness.

"Let's go!" Zeke cries. He dashes toward the tunnel.

"Wait!" you shout. But Zeke has already run inside.

You can't let your friend explore the tunnel alone. You jam the telescope into your shirt and run after him.

Run to PAGE 57.

With a bone-crushing thud, the two of you hit a hard stone floor. You gaze up at the dim light from the basement.

"The secret door!" you shout. "It's sliding shut!"

But there's nothing you can do to stop the door from banging closed. It's too far away.

You glance around. The walls are hard and smooth as glass. There's no way out.

You're trapped.

"We must have made a mistake," you groan. "We'll never get out of here!"

"Don't panic," Zeke tells you. "Maybe someone else will find the diary and open the door."

"Yeah," you reply grimly. "Maybe in another two hundred years."

You scan the bare room. Nothing to eat. Nothing to drink.

And nothing to do.

Nothing to do for *two hundred years*!

Well, you thought living in Swamp House was going to bore you to death.

It looks as if you were right!

THE END

"If there really is a treasure, I bet this book will give us a clue," you declare. "Let's read it!"

Zeke puts down the telescope and peers over your shoulder. You struggle to get the strap off the journal.

"Be careful!" Zeke warns.

Whoops! Too late. You yank a little too hard on the strap. The book flies open. Pages scatter everywhere.

"Oh, no!" you groan.

"Look!" Zeke cries. "The first page is still there."

Sure enough, the first page is still stuck to the binding. As Zeke scoops up the loose pages, you begin to read out loud.

Read on to PAGE 16.

"Maybe we should explore the ship tomorrow when it's light," you tell Zeke. "We could try to move farther away from the river and build a campfire tonight."

"Are you chicken?" Zeke taunts. Then he hauls himself onto the deck of the ship. He dashes up a staircase to one of the upper decks.

"I am *not* chicken," you snap.

With a shudder, you climb aboard. Carefully you follow Zeke up the old, rotten stairs.

"Zeke?" you call.

But he doesn't answer. As you reach the upper deck, you see why. Two men are holding him. A third has his hand clasped over Zeke's mouth.

And there's something very strange about the men. They're dressed in old-fashioned clothes. And all three have extremely pale faces. Too pale.

With a shiver, you realize that you can see right through them. They must be members of the *Annabelle*'s ghost crew!

You want to run away, as far from this ship as you can get!

But you're so scared, you can't move!

Turn to PAGE 96.

Zeke has transformed again. The pale, skeleton-like face is gone. He has the face of a human boy! But his body and clothes are still transparent, almost like glass.

"I'm free!" he shouts, and his voice sounds like the old Zeke.

His face looks so happy. You've seen Zeke smile before, but never like this. You feel glad that you've freed Zeke from his restless wandering in Stinkeye Swamp.

"How can I thank you?" Zeke exclaims.

"Well," you hint, "you did mention something about a treasure."

Turn to PAGE 125.

I can't leave Zeke! you think.

Your back presses against the railing. You feel the cylinder of the brass telescope in your back pocket. Without thinking, you pull it out.

The ghosts shrink back in fright.

They're scared of it! you realize. Frantically, you wave the scope at them.

The ghosts drop back even farther, their eyes wide with fear.

"That telescope belonged to their captain," Zeke shouts. "They're frightened of it!"

With a ferocious roar, you run toward the ghosts who are still holding Zeke. They turn and flee, howling madly. In an instant, they all vanish into the shadows.

"You saved me!" Zeke runs up to join you. "They really hate me."

"They hate you?" you ask.

Zeke gives you a strange look. "I guess since you saved me, I owe you one. It's time for me to tell you the truth."

Hear all about it on PAGE 32.

"Aaaaahhh!" you shriek. You wriggle around in the gunk, struggling to get loose.

But the sewage holds you like glue.

As you inch closer to the huge processing vats you have one comforting thought: Your parents use Green Thumb fertilizer. So at least you might wind up back home.

On the other hand, you'll be spread out on the garden.

"I always recycle!" you groan. "But this stinks!"

THE END

Zeke smiles sadly. As he does, his face changes. In shock, you watch as it becomes long and gaunt. His skull is covered with a thin layer of flesh. And you can see through his head to the moonlit jungle behind.

His clothes swirl and wave. Zeke is suddenly wearing old-fashioned knickers, a sweater, and a cap.

"Y-y-you're a ghost!" you stammer.

"That's right," Zeke replies. "I'm the cabin boy, Ezekiel. It was I who fell asleep and let the *Annabelle* hit that snag. The rest of the crew cursed me. They won't let me leave this swamp until someone takes my place as lookout. I was going to trick you into doing it. But you're my friend, so I'm letting you go."

You don't know what to say. Zeke is a ghost? How can it be? He's your friend! But suddenly a lot of things make sense. Like why he didn't go to your school. Why he always made excuses when it was your turn to go to his house. Why he never wanted to pig out on chips and candy.

You stand there, unsure of what to do.

"I guess I'm stuck here," the ghost in front of you says. "Unless you can find some other way to break the curse. . . ."

Learn more on PAGE 82.

"How is the ship's clock going to help me?" Zeke wonders aloud. He leads you up to the wheelhouse.

"I don't know," you answer. "But let's take a look."

Inside the damp and rotten wheelhouse, Zeke shows you the ship's clock. It's a battered, rust-covered wreck. Springs pop out the back. Both hands point to six o'clock.

"This thing hasn't worked in years," Zeke complains as you poke at the brass clock.

You're about to give up when you notice a small wooden handle on one side.

"What's this for?" you ask. You start turning it.

As you do, you feel your skin start to tingle. Then strange waves of energy slam into you. You glance down.

You are becoming transparent!

Turn to PAGE 92.

"Okay," you tell Zeke. "You're right. Better safe than sorry. Let's go up on the wheelhouse and take a look around."

You and Zeke climb a rickety ladder up the side of the boat. You pass two more decks. Finally you're on top of the wheelhouse.

Underneath you is the spot where the captain stood to steer the boat. You grab on to the thin railing and peer down.

No ghosts — at least, none that you can see.

You start turning to look for Zeke. But you can't.

Your hands! They feel as if they've been caught in rock-hard cement.

"Zeke!" you shout in fear. "Something's wrong! I can't move!"

You suddenly sense someone standing right behind you. You turn your head, just enough to see Zeke. He shimmers in the moonlight. His dark eyes look bottomless. And you can see right through him.

Uh-oh.

Try to move to PAGE 86.

You reach out and grab a card. You close your eyes and force yourself to turn it over. You open one eye.

Oh, no! It's the ace of hearts!

You lose!

You suddenly feel yourself rising through the air, carried by an unseen force. The card flutters to the floor. Ezekiel flies beside you. He has a wide grin on his ghostly face.

"Never gamble with an old riverboat hand," he shouts with glee. "You must take my place as the lookout! Forever!"

You are drawn through the air to the roof of the wheelhouse. Invisible bonds lash you to the railing. You struggle, but you can't get free.

"Thank you!" Ezekiel cries as he flies into the night. "And don't worry. You can get someone else to take your place. Just make friends with the next kid to move into Swamp House!"

How am I supposed to make friends with the next kid if I can't even move? you think.

"Hey! This isn't fair! *You* weren't tied up!" you shout, as you struggle to get loose.

Zeke hovers for a minute. "Good point," he says. "I guess you *can't* get someone else to take your place. So long!"

THE END

"Hubert!" Annabelle screams.

You and Zeke cover your ears.

"Hubert was dancing!" Annabelle explains. "With that prissy, stuck-up Kirsten Mann! I saw them through the window."

"So what?" Zeke mutters. "I thought it was something terrible — like a vampire or something."

Annabelle sighs. "I turned and ran back to the tunnel." She sniffles a little. "But I was so upset, I got lost. And that was when I stumbled onto the treasure. And the curse began!"

This is getting *good*! you think.

Annabelle lowers her voice to a croak. "A skeleton was guarding the treasure! It grabbed me! It said, 'At last, I can rest. *You* will take my place!'"

Annabelle moans. "For two hundred years I have guarded the treasure. But there is a way to break this curse that binds me. If you break the curse, I will give you the treasure. But if you try and then fail, you will have to pay the price."

Help Annabelle break the curse on PAGE 41.
If you think it's too dangerous, turn to PAGE 51.

"That guy looks weird," Zeke comments as you peer at the man in rags.

"But he's closer," you point out. "Come on!"

You trot along the edge of the lake, sometimes splashing into the shallow water. As you get closer, you shout and wave. But the man with the beard doesn't seem to notice you — he just keeps staring at some plants growing by the water's edge.

"Hey, mister!" you call when you're only a few yards away.

The man's head jerks up like a frightened animal. He spots you. Then he darts into the underbrush and disappears!

"Great," Zeke cries. "We lost him. Now what?"

"He can't have gone far," you say.

There's a very faint path into the jungle where the strange man disappeared. By ducking low you can make your way through the heavy growth.

"Hurry up!" you shout over your shoulder as you rush in.

Something under your foot suddenly gives. Your body crashes through a fake floor covered with old leaves.

You're falling!

Land on PAGE 67.

Zeke is already paddling like crazy for the opposite side of the pool. You quickly swim after him.

But it's no use. The goldfish easily keep up with you. You feel a sharp pain in your leg as the first one takes a bite.

"It's no use!" Zeke screams. "They're all around us."

You glance into the water. And gasp.

Staring at you is a very familiar-looking goldfish. It has a black spot around its right eye — the exact shape of California.

"Sparky?" you cry.

The goldfish's mouth opens and closes in an O.

"Sparky!" It's the goldfish you won at a carnival last year! For a week he was your favorite pet.

Then your family went on vacation. You forgot to drop off Sparky at your neighbor's house.

When you got back...well, Sparky wasn't swimming quite as fast as he used to. In fact, he was sort of *floating*. So you sort of flushed him down the toilet.

But Sparky is okay after all! In fact, he looks fit as a fiddle! With a healthy appetite! What great news!

Sparky digs his teeth into your arm. Your leg. Your big toe.

Hmmm. Maybe that part about the healthy appetite isn't such good news. In fact, it's

THE END.

You read more of the instructions:

Start at the stairs. Move from stone to stone, in any direction, including diagonally. You may only move to equal or higher numbers. And you may not stand on the same stone twice. Follow the directions and you'll find the entrance. Fail — and beware!

Open door A and go to PAGE 14.
Open door B and go to PAGE 124.

"L-l-look!" Zeke stammers, grabbing your arm and shaking it. He points to the walls of the pit.

You see that the walls are crawling with giant scorpions.

You watch in horror as they begin scuttling down the sides and out of cracks in the walls. There must be thousands of them! And each one has a long, poisonous stinger.

"Why did I listen to you, Zeke?" you moan.

Turn to PAGE 52.

"Just tell us how to break the curse!" you exclaim.

"Come with me," Annabelle replies.

You and Zeke stumble after the glowing ghost through a maze of tunnels.

The ghost suddenly stops. She waves her hand once. Old-fashioned lamps light up with flickering blue flames.

You are in a huge room. All you can see through its windows are mud and tree roots. Wow! This house sank into the swamp!

"Is this the ballroom where Hubert danced with that other girl?" you ask.

"Yes," Annabelle answers. "And the key to breaking the curse is hidden here! But I can't show it to you."

You peer around the room. Shadows dance in the corners. There's not much in here except a table. A music box sits on it.

"That old music box — does it have something to do with the curse?" you ask Annabelle.

"I'm not allowed to *tell* you anything," she insists. "That's part of the curse. You know, along with being creepy and mean."

But while she speaks, she's nodding her head vigorously and waving her hand at the music box!

Gee. Could she be giving you a hint?

Check out the music box on PAGE 71.

"Let's go through the tree," you shout. "We can climb up it if we have to."

You take off down the right-hand path. When you glance back a minute later, there is no sign of the gator.

You pass through the carved-out trunk of the huge old tree. You've never seen such a big tree in your life!

Soon you're standing on the riverbank next to the wreck of the *Annabelle*. The low bow of the ship juts out over the land at a crazy angle. Its old smokestacks are rusted, and one has a bird's nest on it.

The sun has gone down, and darkness is closing in over the swamp. You don't want to stand on the path any longer. The gator that chased you probably has friends.

But as you gaze at the rusted hulk of the *Annabelle*, you suddenly don't want to climb aboard, either. Treasure or no treasure, the wrecked ship is creepy!

Turn to PAGE 28.

The weird ghost girl floats ahead. You and Zeke stumble after her like puppets on a string.

"Where is she taking us?" you whisper. "What does she mean, our 'doom'?"

"I don't know," Zeke murmurs. "She's under some kind of curse. Maybe we're under a curse now too. Whatever you do, don't get her angry. She has very strong powers."

You nod. The last thing you want to do is get a ghost mad at you!

As you are drawn along the tunnel, you see something round and glittering on the floor. It looks like a jewel — a jewel the size of a baseball.

It must be part of the treasure!

You want to bend over and pick it up. But what if Annabelle sees you? Will that make her angry?

Do you dare pick up the jewel?

If you dare, pick up the jewel on PAGE 72.
If you don't, go to PAGE 131.

You lift the cup on the right and slowly put it to your lips. If this is a magical potion, you think, let it be the one that makes me rich!

You sip. The liquid inside tastes sweet and cold and faintly of bananas. You hand it to Zeke, and he drinks too.

"Yummmm," he says. "A banana shake."

"OOOKA OOKA!" you reply.

Zeke looks at you and drops the cup.

"Y-y-you're . . . ," he stammers.

"OOK? EEKA?" you babble. You meant to ask, "What are you staring at?" But your mouth isn't cooperating!

You look back at Zeke — and gasp! Brown fur sprouts all over his body! His ears grow big, and he shrinks down to the size of a monkey. In fact, he *is* a monkey. You realize what Zeke was trying to tell you — the same thing just happened to you.

"What cute monkeys you make!" Annabelle squeals. She holds out a banana. "Come, monkey. Come get Annabelle's treasure!"

Zeke the monkey scrambles onto Annabelle's shoulder and grabs the banana.

"Save some for me," you try to say.

But all that comes out is "EEKA OOKA!"

THE END

"Don't be such a baby," you scold. "A little dirty water won't hurt you."

You sit on the ledge and slide into the pool. The water is slimy and cold, and your feet don't touch the bottom.

"Come on," you order Zeke. You push off and begin paddling for the other side. You hear a splash as Zeke joins you in the water.

As your hands cut the water's surface, your eyes widen in amazement. "Whoa!" you cry. "The water — it's glowing!"

Use the light to find your way to PAGE 102.

"I'm innocent?" Zeke gasps.

A low murmur rises from the other ghosts.

You hold the captain's log overhead so all of the crew can see it.

"This is your captain's log!" you tell them in a strong, loud voice. "It says right here that Zeke was *not* supposed to be on duty that night. It wasn't his job to be the lookout. So it wasn't his fault that the ship hit a snag!"

"All this time I was innocent?" Zeke asks sadly.

"Yes!" you declare. "The captain blamed you to cover his own mistake." You glare at the crew. "I demand that you release Zeke from your curse," you cry.

There is whispering, almost too low for you to hear. Then one of the ghosts steps forward. He points to Zeke.

"Go!" he moans. The other crew members repeat the call until they sound like a ghostly wolf pack howling at the moon.

"Go! Go! Go!" they moan and shriek.

You turn to Zeke — and almost drop the telescope in shock.

Take a look at him on PAGE 29.

"What are you?" you cry. You struggle to break Ed's grip.

But he's too powerful. You feel as if your arm is going to come off.

"I'm your worst nightmare," the deathly creature replies. "I'm a ghoul. Did I forget to mention that when we first met?"

"A gh-ghoul?" you squeak.

You knew there was something weird about Ed. But you never would have guessed he's a horrifying monster!

You feel as if you're caught in a bad dream. If only you could wake up!

But this is all too real. Ed starts to pull you along the tunnel.

"I got lost down here and died twenty years ago," he explains. "But I'm not a ghost. I'm a ghoul. Which means I still need to eat."

"Eat?" you echo in a meek voice. "What do you eat?"

"One guess," Ed cackles.

You have no choice. Turn to PAGE 91.

48

Keeping one eye on Billings, you slide the note-book back into the pack. You crawl to where Zeke is sound asleep on the ground.

"Zeke," you whisper, nudging him. "Get up. We have to get out of here!"

"Huh?" Zeke mumbles. You cover his mouth with your hand. You signal for him to follow you. The two of you creep quietly away from the campfire.

"What is it?" Zeke asks after you tiptoe down the path. "What's wrong?"

Breathlessly, you tell him what you read in Billings's notebook.

"A witch?" Zeke frowns. "That's crazy."

"Why?" you ask. "The telescope is real, isn't it?"

"That's true," Zeke agrees. "Hey. If Billings can use it to find Annabelle, then we can too!"

"That's right," you agree. "And then *we* can drink her magical potion and we'll be rich and powerful. And we'll live forever!"

You raise the telescope to your eye.

See the sights on PAGE 75.

"Too bad you had to use that on me," Zeke says. Trembling with fear, you lower the telescope. Zeke still appears as a ghost!

"Who are you?" you stammer.

"Ezekiel Smith," comes the whispered reply. "Cabin boy for the *Annabelle*. It was I who fell asleep long ago and let her crash. Now I'm doomed to stay in this rotting swamp. I can only leave if someone takes my place. That's why I brought you here."

"Why me?" you ask, backing away.

"The curse keeps me from leaving this miserable place," he explains. "But you live in Swamp House, just inside the swamp's borders. That's why I was able to talk to you and trick you into coming here. Now you must take my place."

You *were* scared of the ghostly creature. But now you are scared and *angry*. You thought Zeke was your good friend. Maybe your best friend. He tricked you!

"I won't do it!" you shout defiantly. "You were supposed to be my friend!"

"That's true," Zeke answers. "So I'll give you one chance to escape. It's a challenge."

Take the challenge on PAGE 121.

You reach out and seize the blue jewel. For a moment it feels solid in your hand. Then it vanishes.

"You chose wrong!" Zeke wails.

"Quiet!" Annabelle commands. "That's the right jewel." Then her expression softens, and she sounds more like a regular girl.

"Sorry about the gruesome ghost act," she tells you. "It's all part of the curse."

"Y-y-y-you're the Annabelle of the legend?" you stammer.

The teenage ghost nods her head and sighs. "I used to be like you," she explains. "A long time ago. But I did something dumb. And all because of a boy named Hubert.

"My parents didn't like him. They ordered me to stay away from him. So the night of the big ball, my parents locked me in the house!

"I was miserable! The hours went by. Then I remembered the smugglers' tunnels. Even back then there were rumors of hidden treasure under the house."

You stare at Annabelle. You still can't believe you're talking to a ghost!

Hear the rest of the story on PAGE 106.

Did you really turn to this page?

Are you *kidding*?

Come on!

All right, maybe it is risky. After all, if you try to break the curse and then you mess up, you'll be doomed to roam the tunnels for eternity, or something like that. But who says you're going to mess up?

Where's your fighting spirit?

You turned to this page by accident.

Right?

Right.

So pretend this never happened and turn to page 41. Where you really meant to go.

Well? What are you waiting for? Get over to PAGE 41!

The deadly scorpions creep closer.

I should have paid more attention in math class, you think. Then I could have figured out Carl's stupid riddle myself.

You decide to make an educated guess about how many times you're going to get stung. You quickly count the number of scorpions in a square foot. Then you guess how many square feet there are in the pit. You multiply that number by the number of scorpions in one square foot. That's the total number of scorpions in the pit. You divide that in half, because you figure only half of them will actually sting you.

Okay, ready for some good news and some bad news?

The bad news is, you're about to be stung by *a lot* of big, fat, very nasty scorpions.

The good news is, you're not so bad at math, after all!

THE END

Zeke rushes back. "Why did you shut the door?" he demands.

"I didn't shut it!" you reply angrily. "It slammed shut by itself. And look. There's no doorknob on this side!"

You both try to pry the door open, but it's stuck fast.

"Well, we can't get back in," Zeke grumbles, shrugging. "So let's look for the treasure."

"That's what we came for," you agree, trying to sound brave. "Besides," you add, "this tunnel has to lead *somewhere*. There must be another exit."

You and Zeke step forward carefully, guided by the weak light of the old flashlight. The tunnel slopes down. Its walls and ceiling are shaped like an arch. You thought they'd be damp and rough, but instead they're smooth and dry. It's almost as if you're still in your basement. You begin to feel less nervous.

"Hey, this isn't so bad," you comment as you walk.

"Could be worse," Zeke agrees. Then he suddenly flings his arm at you, smacking you hard in the stomach!

Hold your stomach and turn to PAGE 8.

Zeke doesn't answer. Instead, a slow, cold smile spreads across his face. He rises into the air and joins Annabelle near the cavern ceiling.

You stare up at them, quaking in fear.

"Annabelle is my sister," Zeke says at last. "On the night of the ball two hundred years ago, I wanted to play a trick on her. So I followed her into the tunnels. On the way in, I took the knob from the door to the basement. But I lost it. And we were trapped in here."

As you listen, your mind races. Maybe you can pit Zeke and Annabelle against each other! You can escape while they fight!

"Oh, so the curse is all your fault, Zeke," you call.

"Who asked for your opinion?" Zeke screams.

"Calm down," Annabelle orders him. "A mortal child returned the doorknob, just as the curse demands."

"That's true." Zeke holds up the jewel-like globe you found on the cavern floor. "*This* is the doorknob. The curse said it had to be handed to one of us by a mortal child."

"Wow!" you say. "Good thing I came along. Or the dumb trick you played on your sister could have kept you here forever."

Zeke glares at you. "Mind your own business," he snarls.

Maybe he'll calm down on PAGE 15.

"Quit complaining," Zeke whispers. "He has to know his way around here better than we do. Besides," he adds with a gleam in his eye, "maybe he does know how to find the treasure!"

Ed leads you through the tunnels, turning right and then left, back and forth, without pausing.

Finally he leads you into a big room with bright electric lights and a concrete floor. He stops.

A large manhole cover is set into the middle of the floor. You see blue chalk markings on it. At the far end of the room is a steel door, with markings in green chalk.

Ed stares at the manhole cover and then at the steel door.

"Hmm," he mumbles, stroking his dirty beard. "I think those blue marks are the ones I left to tell me how to get back to the treasure. Or are they the ones we made when we were building the sewage plant? I can't remember."

"Great," Zeke mutters. "Which way do we go now?"

There's no way to know which is the right way. So just choose one!

If you go through the manhole, go to PAGE 114.
If you go through the door, go to PAGE 107.

"Heads! This way!" you cry, leading Zeke down the main path. "I'm pretty sure this is the path that leads to town. Hurry! He's right behind us!"

You race down the path. Suddenly, you trip on a tree root — and you're flying through the air!

You land painfully on something hard. Zeke lands next to you. You struggle to get up, but you can't move. You're both stuck to a cluster of heavy vines that crisscross the ground. The vines are covered with a thick, sticky sap. It's holding you tight, sort of like flypaper.

"What is this stuff?" Zeke yells.

"Those are strangler vines," Billings's voice calls. "You're stuck in their sap. It's quite powerful!"

Billings steps to the edge of the path. He caught up! And now he's watching you — the way a spider watches a fly caught in its web.

Try to get loose on PAGE 58.

"Wait up, Zeke!" you shout as you grope your way along the dark tunnel. Suddenly you step into thin air! You're falling through space!

"Help!" you manage to squeak. A second later you splash into ice-cold water. A strong current sucks you under! You fight for your life in the cold, wet darkness.

Finally you struggle to the surface and burst free, gasping for air.

"Zeke!" you croak.

"Over here," comes his faint reply.

The two of you rush along on a fast-flowing underground river. As your eyes get used to the dark, you can see dim outlines. There's Zeke, bobbing in the frigid water just ahead of you.

"I don't know how long I can last!" you shout. You've swallowed a lot of water, and your arms are growing tired.

"Grab that log!" Zeke shouts back.

A long, flat shape is floating by a few feet away. You might be able to reach it. Then you see something up ahead, a vine or a branch hanging down from above.

You have only seconds to choose. Quick! Grab one!

Reach for the branch on PAGE 93.
Lunge for the log on PAGE 19.

"That sap is stronger than glue," Billings announces with an evil grin. "Even a bear can't get loose."

"Help us!" Zeke shouts.

"I don't think so. But I *will* help myself," he answers.

Careful not to touch any of the vines, Billings tiptoes up to you. He reaches into your back pocket and plucks out the brass telescope.

"Ever since I ran into you kids I've been trying to figure out how to get this," he explains. "And how to get rid of you. But you solved my problem for me. Now I can find Annabelle's treasure — by myself!"

You strain with all your might to get up. But you can't move an inch. In fact, the harder you struggle, the more you stick.

Your heart sinks as you realize that Billings is right. You'll never get free!

"What about us?" Zeke shouts as Billings disappears.

"Well, you can't come with *me*!" his voice floats back. "So why don't you just . . . *stick around*?"

THE END

"Going to the wheelhouse is a waste of time," you say. "I want to hunt for the treasure now."

You stroke the gleaming scope and reread the words etched on its side:

To See What Isn't There

This is the key to finding the treasure aboard the *Annabelle*!

You lift the telescope to your eyes.

"No!" Zeke shouts.

Then you see him through the scope. Only . . . Zeke's body waves and shimmers in the light. He's dressed in old-fashioned clothing.

You nearly drop the scope.

Zeke is a ghost!

"Zeke!" you scream.

Take another look on PAGE 49.

The safe is filled to the brim with gold bars!

Yes! you think. There's enough here to buy a dozen houses in your old neighborhood!

You run your fingers over the chunky golden bricks. You can hardly believe it. You outwitted a ghost! And now you're rich!

"Since you won fair and square," Ezekiel says, "I'll help you get the gold home."

He sounds sad. Suddenly you remember that even though he's a ghost, he's still your friend.

"I'm sorry you're still stuck here," you tell him. "Maybe someday we can break that curse and set you free."

"That would be great!" he exclaims, perking up a little. "Till then, can I still visit you? I love playing your video games."

"Okay." You nod. You lift up a gold brick.

"This is going to buy a lot of video games!"

THE END

The two of you run through the clearing and back along the path.

"There's a branch up ahead that leads home," you explain as you hurry along. "It should be close."

Then you come to a dead stop. The main path, wide and level, goes to the left. To the right is a narrow track. It's almost completely overgrown.

"Which way?" Zeke asks.

At the same moment you hear Billings calling you.

"Kids!" he shouts. "Why did you run off?"

"Quick!" Zeke whispers. "Before he catches up! Which way do we go?"

You remember that one of the paths leads to the strangler vines. You don't know what those are, but they don't sound good.

"Hey, you kids! Where are you?" You hear Billings calling you. Then you hear his footsteps thudding along the path.

Which branch is the right one? You're so scared, you can't think. At this point, you might as well flip a coin!

Hey. That's not a bad idea. Flip a coin.

Heads, take the main path on PAGE 56.

Tails, branch off on the smaller path on PAGE 109.

You make your decision. Ed may be nuts, but he seems to know his way around.

I'll catch up with him, you think. Then we can look for Zeke together.

You run down the tunnel in the direction of Ed's voice. It's very dark, but you think you see some lights ahead.

You hurry on. In the next moment you see Ed. He's standing under the dim light of a single bulb.

"Ed, am I glad to see you!" you cry as you rush up to him. "I thought I lost you."

"We wouldn't want that to happen, would we?" Ed mutters.

His voice sounds strange. You start to draw back from him. But he reaches out and roughly grabs your arm.

"What are you doing?" you shout.

He doesn't answer, but the look on his face fills you with dread.

Turn to PAGE 94.

"Zeke, I get the feeling we shouldn't be on this path once it's dark out," you tell him.

He glances at the reptile that's been trailing you.

"I know what you mean," he replies. "But where can we go that's safe?"

Just as Zeke stops speaking, you spot something jutting out of the water downstream.

"What is that?" Zeke cries as you both get closer.

In the red light of the setting sun, you can just make out a huge black shape in the river.

Get even closer on PAGE 68.

"I'm tired of getting wet too," you complain. "Besides, who knows what's swimming in that muck?"

It takes several minutes to reach the log bridge. But finally you step onto the wide, mossy log.

"Hey, look at me!" you shout as you inch across. "I should be in the circus!"

The log shifts suddenly under your feet.

"Quit rocking the log!" you shout over your shoulder.

"I didn't rock anything," Zeke shouts back. You turn your head and see that he's still standing on the bank.

"Well, don't tell me this log moved all by itself," you yell. And then the log does just that — moves by itself!

"That's no log!" Zeke screams. "It's an alligator!"

You glance down. Uh-oh. Zeke is right!

The gator rolls over and throws you into the muck. The giant reptile must be over twenty feet long. It whips around and opens its massive jaws. It has rows of long yellow fangs. You can't escape.

I wonder how he got so big, you think, just before the gator's jaws snap down.

Then it hits you — he eats really well!

LATER, GATOR!

You're about to grab the crowbar, when the safety signs on the wall give you an idea. You snatch up the hard hat and wave it in the air.

"Ed!" you say in a stern voice. "I'm ashamed of you!"

"Why?" Ed frowns. "Because I'm a ghoul?"

"No. Because you're not following sewer safety rule number one!"

You point at the largest sign on the wall. It reads:

SEWER SAFETY RULE NUMBER ONE
ALWAYS WEAR A HARD HAT!

"You're right!" Ed confesses, looking embarrassed. "I always forget that one. Give me that hard hat!"

He grabs for the hat. As he does, you toss it into the open manhole.

Without hesitating, Ed dives after it. Then he screams with rage. The sound trails off into the blackness below.

"Yes!" you cry, pumping your fist in the air. You grab the heavy iron lid. You push it over the manhole until it drops into place. Then you shove the massive table on top of the manhole cover.

"Safety first," you say, rubbing your hands together.

Go to PAGE 95.

You walk in the direction of Zeke's voice.

A light up ahead makes it easier to find your way through the tunnel. You even manage to run a little.

"Zeke!" you shout. "Where are you?"

Soon you find yourself in a large cavern. In the center hangs a brilliant white light. Underneath you spot the slumped over figure of Zeke. You rush toward him.

Then you discover why he hasn't answered. That glow doesn't come from an electric light.

It's the eerie, shining light of a ghost!

The ghost appears to be a young teenage girl. She floats above Zeke, waving her pale arms back and forth. Her long hair streams out wildly behind her.

She turns toward you. You feel the black holes of her eye sockets burn into you. Your heart pounds and your legs shake.

"Hello," she greets you in a voice that sounds like a hurricane. "Won't you come in? I am Annabelle."

Turn to PAGE 10.

Your stomach turns as you tumble into a deep pit.

THUMP!

You land on a musty pile of leaves. A second later Zeke lands next to you. Both of you sit up and brush yourselves off.

You're bruised — but nothing seems broken.

"Are you okay?" you ask Zeke.

"Yeah," he grunts. "What happened?"

"I think we fell into a trap." You stand up. The sides of the pit are steep, and the top is yards above.

"Give me a boost," you tell Zeke. "Maybe I can climb up."

Before your friend can move, a man's head appears over the rim of the pit.

Turn to PAGE 23.

As you walk closer, you can make out the rotting hulk of an old paddle-wheel steamboat. It's sitting at a crazy angle, on the very edge of the river. It's covered with moss and vines.

"It's got to be the *Annabelle*," you insist.

"Come on, let's go!" Zeke shouts, tugging at your arm. "I can almost smell the treasure!"

"And we'll be safe on board," you chime in. "But which way?"

The path splits in two just ahead — then joins again farther down. The branch on the left goes under some vines dotted with beautiful bright red flowers. The path on the right goes right through the trunk of a huge old tree.

The alligator suddenly swims faster. It lunges out of the water behind you! And, boy, can it move!

Quick! Choose a path!

Go under the vines on PAGE 84.
Go through the tree on PAGE 42.

Your hand trembles as you pick up the cup on the left. You take a small sip.

It's delicious!

"It tastes just like chocolate milk!" you say.

"Let me have some!" Zeke demands. You hand him the cup, and he slurps the rest down.

"Good choice," Annabelle says approvingly.

"Does that mean we passed the test?" you ask eagerly. "Now will you give us the treasure, after all?"

"Treasure?" Annabelle laughs. "Not a chance. Passing the test simply means that I won't turn you into flowerpots."

"Flowerpots?" You gulp.

"That's right." Annabelle gives you a sly grin. "But you look like nice kids, so I'm going to show you the way home."

She waves her hand and a string of blue lights appears, leading off through the swamp.

"Just follow those and you'll be home by dawn," she says.

"Come on," Zeke urges, as he tugs you toward the lights.

Well, you think, we didn't find the treasure. But we did get a nice cup of chocolate milk. Next time I meet a witch in a swamp, I'll remember to ask for a cookie too.

THE END

Annabelle's terrible voice echoes off the tunnel walls.

"It was here that I left my home many years ago," she declares in a voice like howling wind. "My parents tried to keep me from going to the biggest ball of the season. But I sneaked out through these old smugglers' tunnels. People said they were cursed, but I didn't believe them."

"I danced all night. Then I returned here, only to find that my little brother had played a trick on me — a deadly trick. He removed the doorknob from this side."

"But he tricked himself also. He lost the doorknob, and he was trapped with me. We never found the knob and we never returned home. We died here in these dark caverns. That was the smugglers' curse on people who used these tunnels without their permission. Now our ghosts are doomed to wander here until the curse is lifted."

She points her ghostly hand straight at you.

"You!" she screams. "You can lift the curse!"

Turn to PAGE 112.

You and Zeke walk over to the music box.

You've never seen one so fancy. You open the richly carved lid. Inside, the brass works gleam.

"How does it work?" Zeke asks.

"A cylinder goes here," you explain, pointing to an empty spot. "Each cylinder plays a different song."

"Like these?" Zeke asks. He picks up two brass rods from the table. You notice little labels on the cylinders. One reads: MIDNIGHT WALTZ. The other says COME-BACK TANGO.

"If this music box has something to do with the curse," you reason, "then the song it plays might be important."

Zeke studies the cylinders. "The curse started at midnight," he declares. "Play 'Midnight Waltz.'"

"But Annabelle made us 'come back' to the ballroom where it all began," you point out. "Maybe 'Come-Back Tango' is the right song."

Which do you play?

If you play "Midnight Waltz," go to PAGE 79.
If you play "Come-Back Tango," go to PAGE 118.

You can't resist. That jewel could be worth a fortune! You bend over and scoop it up. You jam it into your pocket.

Annabelle still moves noiselessly up ahead. She didn't seem to notice. You breathe a sigh of relief.

Your sigh almost turns into a cry of fear when you feel something poke you in the side.

"Take it easy," Zeke whispers. "It's just me. What was that? What did you find?"

You start to tell him, but Annabelle turns around and directs her terrible stare right at you. You freeze with fear.

If I tell him, Annabelle might hear, you think.

But what if the jewel is some kind of clue to the curse? Zeke could help you figure out what it means.

Should you try to whisper to him?

Whisper to Zeke on PAGE 78.
Keep quiet on PAGE 6.

"Swim? In that?" Zeke stares at the filthy water.

"Do you have a better idea?" you ask. "Look. There's another tunnel across the pool. We can't go back up, so that's the only way out."

Zeke points. "I think this ledge goes all the way around."

You peer through the darkness. The ledge gets narrower as it winds around the pool. It seems to stop halfway. But it's hard to tell with your flashlight's weak beam.

"We can't make it that way," you object. "It's too narrow. And those rocks over the ledge look loose. What if they fall on us?"

"It's better than swimming in that gunk," Zeke replies.

You gaze at the gross water. He has a point.

You have to get across, but how?

Do the backstroke to PAGE 45.
Or edge along the ledge to PAGE 12.

You and Zeke gobble up a couple of candy bars that Ranger Billings pulls out of his pack. Then he leads you onto one of the narrow paths crisscrossing the swamp.

The path twists and turns and almost disappears a couple of times. But the ranger seems sure of the way.

"This path leads out of the swamp," he explains. "But it's easy to get lost, so stick by me. After I get the soil samples tomorrow, I'll bring you straight home."

The day drags on as you slog behind the ranger through the endless swamp. From time to time he stops to let you rest. On one of those stops you notice him writing in a small black notebook. You walk to where he is sitting and glance over his shoulder.

Ranger Billings sees you and snaps the book shut. But before he does, you see one word: Annabelle!

Billings said he was here to collect soil samples! Why is he writing about Annabelle?

"Annabelle?" you blurt out. "Like the legend of Annabelle?"

Billings's eyes blaze with anger.

"Who told you to poke around?" he shouts angrily.

Turn to PAGE 108.

When you hold the scope to your eyes, a trail marked by magic blue lights appears. The lights twinkle in the dark swamp.

The two of you follow the trail. Before long, you come to a small clearing flooded by bright moonlight. A tiny hut sits at the base of a towering old tree. Inside the hut, a small fire is burning.

A dark figure appears in the doorway. You know without asking that it's Annabelle. She's dressed in a flowing black robe, and her gray hair reaches almost to the ground.

"Who's out there?" she calls.

You and Zeke stand as still as you can. Maybe she won't see you.

"Come closer," she calls. "I know you are there. I *smell* you. I can *always* smell children. If you don't come closer now, I'll set my dogs on you."

As soon as she says the word "dogs," two huge wolflike creatures bound from the hut. They stand at Annabelle's side, snarling and growling in your direction.

"What should we do?" Zeke asks.

"What *can* we do?" you reply. You step forward. "Hello!" you call out.

Get a little closer on PAGE 127.

There's a bright flash — and the spirit appears in front of you.

"You cannot escape!" the ghost hisses. "I am Annabelle. This is *my* world."

"Leave us alone!" you manage to squeak. "We don't mean you any harm."

"Yes," she replies with a gruesome smile. "But I mean *you* harm. Unless . . ."

"Unless?"

"Unless you can choose correctly," she finishes.

"Choose?" you and Zeke repeat.

Annabelle holds out her bony hands. A jewel shimmers in each palm. One is red. One is blue.

"One means life. The other your doom," she whispers.

Then she sweeps a ghostly arm through the air. In the wake of her arm, eerie letters appear, glowing in the air. She points to them.

"The answer is here," she declares. "Now find it!"

Start looking on PAGE 110.

Carl stares at the telescope as if hypnotized.

"Got that? From where?" he whispers.

You tell him how you and Zeke found the telescope and arrived in the swamp.

You hand him the scope. "So what do you know about this?"

"From the *Annabelle* it is," Carl answers softly as he turns the scope over in his hands.

"Annabelle?" you repeat. "I thought that was a girl."

"No," Carl says thoughtfully. "The *Annabelle.* She was a big paddle-wheel steamboat — a gambling boat. Ran up and down the river a long time ago, she did. Legend says one foggy night, the cabin boy on lookout fell asleep. The *Annabelle* ripped her bottom out on a snag. Sank, she did, and the whole crew went down with her. The crew — and a lot of gamblers' gold. Some say, with the captain's telescope you can find the wreck."

For a long minute you all sit, silently. Then Carl gasps.

"Leave this place! That's my advice!" he shouts, handing back the telescope. He stands up and starts hopping in place.

But you ignore him. All you can think of is the treasure. It really exists! And you can find it!

Start looking for it on PAGE 119.

Maybe if I whisper, she won't hear, you think.

You keep your eyes on Annabelle. You try not to show how scared you are.

Finally she stops staring at you. She flies ahead, leaving you and Zeke alone. You pull the jewel-like globe from your pocket and hand it to him.

"I saw it on the ground," you explain, keeping your voice low. "What do you think it is?"

"I know what it is," Zeke declares. But his voice sounds strange. Scratchy. Distorted.

As you stare at him, his face becomes paler and paler. His eyes grow black. And then you notice he's almost transparent.

You can see right through him!

You want to run away as fast as you can. But your feet are rooted to the ground.

"Sister!" Zeke calls in a terrible, harsh voice.

With a feeling of dread, you realize who he is calling.

The ghost of Annabelle flies back toward the two of you.

"Yes, brother?" she responds with an evil smile.

"We have it at last!" Zeke cries. "The curse is broken!"

"Zeke!" you scream. "*You're* a ghost?"

Turn to PAGE 54.

You pick up the rod labeled MIDNIGHT WALTZ and slip it into place. Then you wind the crank on the outside of the music box. Slowly the cylinder begins to turn. The tinkling notes sound strangely comforting in the dark, eerie ballroom.

"My waltz!"

You whirl around at the sound of Annabelle's voice. Her deathly pale face is contorted in anger.

"You played my waltz!" she cries. "The one I never danced with Hubert!"

Uh-oh.

"She sure is moody," Zeke comments in a low voice.

"Shhhh," you caution him. "We don't want her to get even madder."

Give Annabelle your best smile. Then waltz to *PAGE 117.*

"Stinkeye Swamp isn't haunted," Zeke scoffs. "Those are just dumb stories."

"Haunted or not, how are we supposed to get out of here?" you wonder out loud. "It looks like no human being has ever set foot here."

Just as the words leave your mouth, you see a man hopping along the shore of the lake. He's a few hundred yards away. And he's like no one you've ever seen. He has a white beard practically down to his waist, clothes that are little more than rags, and a hat made out of tree branches.

"Someone's coming!" you tell Zeke.

"I see someone coming from over there!" Zeke says.

You peer in the opposite direction and see another man! This one wears the green uniform of a park ranger. He's much farther away than the man in rags. You and Zeke yell, but neither man seems to notice.

"They're too far away," Zeke says. "We have to run to one of them. But which one?"

Talk to the man in rags on PAGE 37.
Check in with the park ranger on PAGE 113.

Billings snorts and begins talking in his sleep.

"Annabelle," he mumbles. He reaches out and grabs the pack in his sleep.

Oh, no! You can't get the map out again without waking him. You want to wake Zeke and sneak away. But what chance would the two of you have in the swamp at night, without the map?

You crawl to your blanket and try to sleep. In the morning, you act calm. But you're just waiting for a chance to get Zeke alone.

"Okay, kids!" Billings finally says. "Let's go."

You follow Billings and Zeke down the path to a clearing.

"You two stay here," Billings instructs you. "I'm going ahead to get some soil samples."

He walks into an overgrown patch of trees and bushes. As soon as he disappears, you tell Zeke everything you've learned.

"I bet he wants to get the telescope," you finish.

"What should we do?" Zeke asks nervously.

"Let's run for it," you answer. "I'm pretty sure this clearing was on the map. And so was the path we just took."

Escape to PAGE 61.

"Other way?" you repeat. "There's another way to break the curse?" You're still in a daze.

From a small tin chest on deck, Zeke draws out an old parchment scroll. As he unrolls it, bits of yellowed paper flake off the edges.

"This scroll belonged to the captain. He said it could break the curse," Zeke tells you. "But I've never been able to solve the puzzle. Can you? If you do, I'll show you where the treasure is hidden."

Check out the scroll on PAGE 20.

I can't help Zeke here, you think, as the ghosts close in. You grab the rail and throw yourself over, landing with a thud on the ground.

You don't have time to catch your breath before you hear terrible shrieks and screams from above.

"Zeke!" you shout.

I can't leave him, you think. No matter what.

Gathering your courage, you get ready to climb back aboard. Suddenly there's a deathly silence.

"Zeke!" you shout again.

Zeke's familiar face appears above the railing.

"It's okay!" he shouts back. "You can come back now!"

"But the ghosts . . . ," you begin.

"They're gone!" Zeke calls. "Come aboard! What are you waiting for?"

You hear gurgling and swishing in the water. More gators? you think with a shiver.

You don't feel happy about it, but you quickly climb back onto the ship.

Climb back aboard on PAGE 11.

"This way!" you shout, dashing down the left-hand path with the vines. Zeke runs after you. A moment later you think you hear the splash of a disappointed, hungry alligator plopping back into the river.

"Look at those flowers," you say as you pass under the strange-looking vines. "I've never seen anything like them."

"I have," Zeke answers matter-of-factly. "Those plants are Venus flytraps. You know, the plants that eat flies and meat —"

You're about to answer when you feel an iron-hard tendril coil itself around your ankles.

"The plant!" you scream. "It's got me!"

Turn to PAGE 18.

Nervously, you reach out and take a card. With a trembling hand, you turn it over.

Ace of spades! You win!

Zeke stares at you with his dead black eyes.

"You did it," he finally grunts. "You must be lucky!"

"What about the treasure?" you demand.

He points toward a large metal safe against the wall.

You run over, fling open the door, and peer inside.

Find out what's inside on PAGE 60.

Zeke is a ghost!

You're so shocked, you can barely talk.

"Zeke!" you squeak. "Is that you?"

Zeke, or Zeke's ghost, opens its mouth. A low moaning voice comes out.

"Yes, it's me," he wails. "But I'm not who you think I am. I'm Ezekiel Smith, cabin boy of the *Annabelle*. It was I who let her run into trouble and sink. I fell asleep at my watch. The angry crew cursed my spirit. I was bound to this swamp — forced to stand lookout every night — forever. But now I'm free!"

"Free?" You gulp. "How come?"

"I've found someone to take my place!" Zeke declares.

"Um. That's nice. Who did you find?" you ask, dreading the answer.

Find out on PAGE 105.

You slide the map case out of the pack. You've been following Billings all day. But you don't trust him. You want to see exactly where you are!

You silently unroll the map. Holding it up to the light of the campfire, you get your bearings. You find the lake you floated into. There's the trail that Billings led you on.

Billings lied! you realize. He isn't leading us out of the swamp — he's taking us right into the heart of it!

You hold the map closer to the fire, trying to make out the scrawled notes on it. "Get telescope!" says one. "Rent park ranger uniform," says another.

Billings isn't even a real ranger!

Turn to PAGE 17.

Your mouth doesn't seem to be working!

You glance at Zeke. Whoa. He's shrinking!

As you stare, Zeke starts sucking his thumb!

Now you feel yourself shrinking too. The drink *was* magic, you realize in horror. It's turning us into . . .

"Babies. *My* babies!" Annabelle cries. "I always wanted children!" She scoops you both up and holds out a baby bottle of formula.

"Here, babies," she coos. "Here's Annabelle's treasure!"

In spite of yourself, you start crying. You want to tell her that she can't do this to you. You want to demand that she change you back to the way you were.

But most of all you want to tell her that it's time for her to change your diaper.

THE END

The treasure, you decide. The smugglers must have hidden the key to the curse with their treasure!

The curse will be lifted. Annabelle will be happy. And you'll be loaded!

You cross to the door leading to the treasure. "This way," you announce, trying to sound sure of yourself.

"The treasure!" Annabelle screams. Now her voice sounds like the breaking of branches in a hurricane.

"But I . . ." You try to explain that you were only trying to break the curse. But somehow the ghost squeezes the air out of your chest. You can hardly breathe.

"You don't want to help me! You just want to get rich," she shrieks. "If that's all you care about, then go ahead — have the treasure! In fact, stay with it *forever*!"

An invisible hand lifts you up and hurls you through the air. The door opens and you hurtle through, landing on a huge pile of gold coins and gems. Then the door slams shut. You're trapped in the darkness, with mounds of treasure all around you.

And you're part of the hoard. For eternity.

Well, your mom always said you were precious!

THE END

Suddenly it hits you. The curse began when Annabelle left home. To break it, she has to get back into her house. You must open the door to the basement. But how?

You walk to the door, with Zeke and Annabelle hovering behind you. In the glow from Annabelle's light you spot the hole where the doorknob should go. The rest of the door is smooth.

"Without the doorknob we cannot enter," Annabelle wails.

You shove your hand into your pockets as you try to think of a solution. Your hand hits the big jewel you found on the tunnel floor. You pull it out and peer at it more closely.

Hmm. It's not a jewel at all. It's a carved piece of crystal. A metal rod sticks out of one end.

"Hey, maybe this will work," you say. You slip it into the hole in the door. It clicks as it slides into place.

With a trembling hand, you turn the knob. The door swings open. You can see the old basement on the other side.

"The curse is broken!" Annabelle declares. Her voice sounds gentler, almost human. "I am free, thanks to you."

You and Zeke rush toward the door.

"Wait!" Annabelle cries. "As your reward for breaking the curse, I will show you the treasure."

Take it! Take it! Take it on PAGE 97.

The Ed-ghoul drags you down a slimy tunnel into a small room. The walls are plastered with signs that have slogans like SAFETY FIRST!

In the middle of the room is a large wooden table littered with tools, a big flashlight, a lunch box, and blueprints. Just to the side of the table is an open manhole.

This must be Ed's old work site, you realize.

The ghoul throws his shovel and wrench on the table and then turns to you with a hideous grin.

Your heart thumps in your chest. You have to get away. Otherwise, you'll be ghoul food for sure! You glance around for something, *anything* to help you get free.

On the table, just within reach of your free hand, are two objects. One is a construction hard hat.

The other is a heavy steel crowbar.

What do you grab?

If you snatch up the crowbar, go to PAGE 104.
If you grab the hard hat, go to PAGE 65.

"You're turning into a ghost!" Zeke cries.

"Nooo!" you scream.

You grab the clock and hold it up to your face. It has letters on it that you didn't notice before. You squint to make them out:

TIME FLIES

I'll say, you think. I was a kid. And now I'm a ghost!

You're kind of bummed out. It'll be hard to make friends in your new neighborhood now.

But cheer up. At least you have Zeke. For as long as you can stand him. And then some.

THE END

The log is floating by too fast, you think. Gathering your strength, you leap from the water as the river pulls you toward the hanging branch. Your hand closes on it.

"Got it!" you shout. Now you can see that the branch is actually a thin tree root poking down through the dirt from above. For a moment you hang there. You search in the gloom for a sign of Zeke.

"Whoa!" Dirt around the branch crumbles and falls.

Now bigger chunks of dirt and rocks rain down on your head. With a shock you realize that your weight is pulling the entire tree right through the dirt!

Desperately, you try to fling yourself clear as the tree crashes through.

Too late! The tree falls and you plunge into the icy current. You struggle to keep your head above the raging water — but it's no use. You grab the small tree, but it won't hold you up. As you sink, you wrap your arms around its damp bark.

"I'm finished — because of a tree!" you moan. "And to think of all the trees I saved in the school recycling drive. If I ever get out of here, I'm never going to hug a tree again!"

THE END

"Let go!" you yell as Ed's fingers dig into your arm. "You're hurting me!"

"Am I?" Ed responds. Then he lets out a weird laugh.

You glance at his face. And scream in horror.

His flesh is melting!

His whole body is transforming. He's becoming thin and ghostlike, almost transparent. But his hand still grips you with incredible strength. His eyes hang loosely in their sockets. His nose is sliding down his face. You can see his skeleton poking out through his paper-thin skin.

"Why are you screaming?" Ed asks. "Haven't you ever seen a person's face melt off?"

Shake with terror until you reach PAGE 47.

You check out the junk on the table. Right on top is a worn, grease-stained book that reads, *Guide to City Sewers*.

"Perfect!" you cry. You thumb through it. It's full of maps and instructions for getting around in the sewer system. You grab the flashlight from the table and rush back the way you came, yelling for Zeke.

"I'm over here!" you hear him call after a few minutes.

A moment later you find him. Quickly, you tell him what happened. "I don't know about you," you finish, "but I've had enough treasure hunting for today. Let's go home."

"I'm with you," Zeke agrees.

The maps are easy to read. Before long you're climbing up a ladder. You scramble out through a manhole cover.

"We made it!" Zeke shouts happily, climbing out behind you.

"Uh, Zeke . . ." You glance around. "I think that map was a little out of date."

You gulp nervously as a large gorilla lumbers toward you. The map has led you right into its cage at the city zoo!

"He's huge!" Zeke whispers in panic. "Will he hurt us?"

"I h-hope not," you stammer. "Let's hope he just wants to monkey around!"

THE END

96

Two other ghosts suddenly appear and float toward you. They don't speak as they grab for you with their filmy hands.

You're frozen in terror — until Zeke manages to get his mouth free and yell at you.

"Run!" he shouts. "Save yourself! They can't leave the ship!"

You glance over the side of the ship. One leap and you'll be safe on the ground. Maybe if you escape, you can figure out a way to save Zeke.

But that means leaving your friend at the mercy of the ghosts. If you stay, maybe you can help Zeke get away.

Another step and the ghosts will have you. It's now or never!

Escape on PAGE 83.
Try to save Zeke on PAGE 30.

Treasure? Yahoo! you think.

You turn to Annabelle. "Sure. That would be nice."

You and Zeke follow Annabelle down the narrow tunnel to the second door. It's dark, solid-looking wood, held shut by a solid iron lock.

"Only my dear brother can open this door," Annabelle tells you.

"Your brother?" you moan. "Where is he?"

"Right here!" a voice announces.

You turn around.

"Zeke?" you murmur. "*You're* Annabelle's brother?"

Figure it all out on PAGE 101.

"No," you blurt out. "The number of sticks in his hat is three. Add six to that and you get nine. Nine is the answer. The rest of the riddle is just to throw you off."

Carl stares at you for a moment.

"Did it!" he says finally. "Solved the riddle, you did. Carl must keep his word!"

He disappears. A moment later a crude ladder of branches appears over the rim of the pit. Sure enough, it has nine rungs. Soon you and Zeke are standing with Carl at the edge of the trap.

Close up, you see that Carl is even weirder-looking than you thought. He keeps making strange faces — grimacing and widening his eyes.

"Uh, do you think you could show us the way out of here?" you ask timidly.

"Leave so soon?" he replies. "Maybe. But first Carl takes you home for a nice drink of cold water. Come along! Follow Carl!"

"It might be another trap," Zeke whispers.

Zeke could be right.

Then again, Carl did keep his first promise. And you *are* thirsty.

Follow Carl to PAGE 13.

Zeke smiles a terrible smile. You begin to think you made a mistake. You watch as he keeps shuffling the cards.

Moving faster than your eyes can follow, he deals two cards facedown onto the green felt table.

"Choose!" he commands.

The two cards appear identical. You must choose one.

What do you do?

Get a deck of playing cards. Pull out the ace of spades and the ace of hearts. Turn them facedown and shuffle them around. Now pick one.

If you pick the ace of hearts, go to PAGE 35.

If you pick the ace of spades, go to PAGE 85.

"We're not sewer workers," you reply. "We're just lost down here." You glance around. "Are we really in the sewer?"

"Of course you're in the sewer!" The man sounds insulted. "I've been working in sewers for almost twenty years, so I ought to know when I'm in a sewer."

He sticks out his hand, and you find yours being squeezed in a hearty handshake.

"Name's Ed," he tells you. "Repair crew fourteen." He peers at you carefully. "Say, you're not a foreman, are you?"

"No," you tell him, hiding a grin. Can't he see you're just a kid? You and Zeke introduce yourselves.

"Hey," Zeke declares happily, "if you're a sewer worker, and this is the sewer, then you can get us out of here!"

"Nope," Ed says with a shake of his head. "No can do. Sorry."

"Why not?" you ask.

"I'm lost too," Ed replies. "Been lost almost twenty years."

You and Zeke stare at each other.

What is this guy talking about?

Turn to PAGE 7.

"You?" you ask with a shudder. "You're a ghost?"

"Well, duh," Zeke replies. As you watch, he grows almost transparent, like Annabelle.

"You should really pick your friends more carefully," he tells you. "Now let's see about that treasure."

He waves his hand and the massive door swings open. On the other side is a room full of gold coins and jewels.

"It's yours," Zeke informs you as he rises into the air next to Annabelle. "It's your reward for finding the doorknob and breaking the curse. We have no use for it."

"It's the least we can do," Annabelle adds. "So what are you going to do with all this wealth?"

"I was going to buy my old house back and move back to my old neighborhood," you reply. "But now I don't know."

"You mean you want to stay at Swamp House?" Zeke asks.

"Yeah," you answer with a grin. "Because after you two take off, it won't be haunted anymore!"

THE END

You gaze around. The entire cavern lights up with an eerie green glow. And it is definitely coming from the pool.

Zeke pulls alongside you and begins treading water. "It was pitch-black before," he declares. "Why is it glowing now?"

"Because now we're in it?" you suggest. You can't think of any other reason.

"Or maybe it's the goldfish making it glow," Zeke suggests. He peers into the water. "There sure are a lot of them."

Zeke's right. Dozens of fish wriggle around you. "I wonder how they got here —" you begin.

"Yeow!" Your sentence is interrupted by Zeke's cry of pain.

"One of the goldfish!" he yells. "It bit me!"

"Don't be dumb." You laugh. "Goldfish don't have teeth."

Then one of the goldfish in front of you opens its mouth.

It has row after row of tiny, needle-sharp teeth.

"*These* goldfish do!" Zeke shouts. "Swim faster!"

"Wait!" you cry. "We still have a long way to swim. Maybe we should try to frighten them off."

Swim like crazy for PAGE 38.
Try to frighten the goldfish on PAGE 115.

You and Zeke don't even have time to scream as you fall into the pitch-black hole.

WHAM!

Somehow you land feet first on a solid stone ledge. Then something heavy knocks you to the ground.

"Aaahh!" you scream.

"Take it easy." Zeke's voice echoes in the darkness. "It's just me!"

"Wow!" he exclaims as the two of you untangle yourselves. He pulls the flashlight from his pocket and aims it up at the broken ladder. "Why didn't you tell me the ladder was so weak?"

You roll your eyes. Then you grab the flashlight and shine it around you.

You've landed on a wide stone ledge. Just below you the pit is full of water. You can see green pond scum floating on the dirty brown liquid. Small red and gold shapes wriggle in the filthy water.

"Goldfish?" you murmur. You're surprised to see them. But they look kind of cute and familiar in this strange place.

"Ugh. I'm glad we didn't land in that water," Zeke says.

"Don't be too happy," you warn him. "Look around. The only way off this ledge is to swim."

Turn to PAGE 73.

104

You grab the crowbar. In one swift move, you swing it toward the ghoul's face. "YAAAAAAAH-HHH!" you scream.

But Ed reaches out and easily snatches the tool away from you.

"Thanks," he announces. "I was looking for that. That's my toothpick. I'll need it after I'm done. I may be a ghoul, but I believe in good dental hygiene."

Hygiene?

Ed licks his lips and bares his sharp teeth.

Sorry. There's nothing more you can do — except hope you give him cavities!

THE END

"I found YOU!" Zeke's ghostly laugh chills your bones.

"Me? Why me?" you cry, struggling against the magic bonds that hold you tight.

"You lived in Swamp House," Zeke rasps. "You were the only kid in my reach."

"But I don't want to take your place. I don't want to be a ghost!" you wail.

Zeke shrugs. "Sorry. Neither did I."

Then he slowly drifts away across the water.

You try with all your might to let go of the rail, but you can't budge an inch. Zeke is right. You'll never get away.

Well, you always did want to stay up late every night.

You just hope this boat has cable TV!

THE END

"Did you ever go into the tunnels before?" you ask.

Annabelle shakes her head. Her wispy hair flutters around her shoulders. "No," she admits. "But that night I was determined to find out if the rumors were true. Because if there were tunnels leading through the swamp, I could go to the ball and my parents would never know!

"I put on my best gown and ran through the tunnels until I reached the house where the ball was being held. I rushed to the front door. My heart was pounding. I peeped through the windows. And then I saw it."

"Saw what?" you ask breathlessly.

"Terrible! Terrible!" Annabelle wails.

You shudder. What could be so terrible that this ghost is still horrified by it?

Find out on PAGE 36.

"I don't want to go deeper underground," you say. "Let's try the door instead of the manhole."

Ed turns the handle on the heavy steel door. Without waiting for Ed or Zeke, you step inside to have a look.

The floor on the other side is wet and slippery. Before you know it, you're sliding feet first down a steep chute.

"Help!" you scream. You brace yourself for a bone-jarring fall.

Instead you land very gently in a huge pile of something soft and squishy.

"What's that terrible smell?" you wail.

Then you spot a sign on the wall: GREEN THUMB SEWAGE TREATMENT AND FERTILIZER PLANT.

That's why the chalk marks were green, you realize. They marked the entrance to the *Green* Thumb plant. You're up to your neck in manure! Gross!

Then the pile of manure *moves*.

Uh-oh. You're on a conveyor belt.

Just ahead is a huge machine. The door in it gapes open like a huge sewage-eating mouth. You're headed straight for it!

You're about to be turned into fertilizer!

Hold your nose and turn to PAGE 31.

You stare at Billings in shock.

He laughs. "Just kidding! You don't really believe that legend, do you?" he asks. "I'm just writing about my girlfriend — Annabelle."

He stands up and lifts his pack. "Come on, let's go!" he calls out cheerfully.

You and Zeke follow him. As you walk, your mind races. Was Billings really just kidding around? He seemed so angry! And what a strange coincidence that his girlfriend's name is Annabelle.

Finally, Billings leads you into a wide, dry clearing. You and Zeke collapse on the ground while the ranger makes a fire. He whips together a hot stew from some packaged food.

By the time you finish eating, it's dark. Billings gives you each a blanket and then lies down by the fire. In minutes, he and Zeke are snoring.

You know you should go to sleep too. But you're wide awake. By the flickering light of the fire you see that Billings has left his pack open. Right on top is the black notebook. You also see a rolled-up map in a plastic case.

As quietly as you can, you crawl to the pack.

Read the notebook on PAGE 126.
Check out the map on PAGE 87.

"Tails. Let's try this way," you say, pulling Zeke onto the narrow, overgrown path. "I just hope we don't end up in the Strangler Vine Thicket."

You and Zeke struggle through the bushes. Finally, after more than an hour, you stumble wearily onto a dirt road.

Another hour later, the two of you reach town.

When you walk through the kitchen door of Swamp House, your mom drops the dish she was drying and hugs you hard. Then she shakes you. Then she hugs you again.

"Where have you been?" she asks. "We've been worried sick about you!"

Exhausted, you pour out the whole story.

"You've been gone all night, and then you tell me a crazy, made-up story like that?" she demands. "Go to your room. I'm going to start thinking about your punishment."

Oh, no, you think as you climb the stairs. Your mom has a way of hitting you where it hurts. Once, she took away your Nintendo for a month.

You start thinking about the choice you just made: the strangler vines or Mom. The strangler vines or Mom. Hmmm.

Yup.

You should have taken your chances with the strangler vines!

THE END

You stare at the floating letters. They're in the shape of a grid. Like a word search.

Suddenly Annabelle says in a low voice, "Annabelle rules Smugglers' Tunnel. Those uninvited all meet their doom."

She repeats the words over and over.

What does it mean? you wonder.

Then it hits you. "It's a word hunt!" you whisper to Zeke. "We have to find the words Annabelle is saying in that grid floating in the air! I bet you anything the leftover letters will spell out which jewel to choose."

With your finger, you copy the grid in the sand floor and begin to circle the words you find.

Take a look at the grid on PAGE 111. Circle each word from Annabelle's chant. The words go up, down, forwards, and backwards. After you've circled them all, read the leftover letters. Then choose the red jewel or the blue jewel.

ANNABELLE RULES SMUGGLERS' TUNNEL. THOSE UNINVITED ALL MEET THEIR DOOM.

```
C D H S E O O
T E E M L L A
H T R U L E S
E I S G E E T
I V B G B E U
R N M L A S N
L I O E N O N
U N O R N H E
E U D S A T L
```

112

"Me?" you reply, trembling. "How can I remove the curse?"

"Only a living child can break the curse," Annabelle declares. "To do it you must choose the right path."

She waves her arm and another beam of light reveals a second door, down a short tunnel to the left.

"Down that tunnel lies the door to the treasure," she explains. "Open one of these doors to break the curse. It is up to you. Choose wisely!"

You have no idea which door to open to lift the curse.

You glance at the door to your basement. It leads home — even if home is stinky Swamp House! And right now, going home sounds like the best thing in the world. You want to get away from Annabelle and out of these creepy tunnels — as fast as possible!

Then you peer down the short tunnel to the door guarding the treasure. It's so close! And you'd be rich!

A chill travels down your spine. Which one?

"Choose!" Annabelle commands again.

You heard her!

To go to the treasure, turn to PAGE 89.
To go home, turn to PAGE 90.

"I bet you anything that park ranger can get us out of here," you decide. "Let's hurry, before he gets out of sight!"

The two of you rush in the ranger's direction, shouting at the top of your lungs.

The ranger turns and peers at you. He seems very surprised.

"What are you two doing here?" he asks as you and Zeke dash up.

He's tall and broad, with kindly eyes under the brim of his ranger's hat. He introduces himself as Paul Billings.

"Boy, are we glad we found you," you exclaim. You tell him your story, from the time you found the telescope until the moment you saw him. His eyes seem to light up when you mention the telescope. But then a worried look crosses his face.

"I can lead you two home," he tells you. "But I'm gathering soil samples for an environmental test. It's very important that I get them on time. You're going to have to tag along with me for a day until I'm finished."

"That sounds fine to me," Zeke responds. "As long as you know your way out of here."

Get the dirt on PAGE 74.

"Let's go into the manhole," you tell Ed. "You said the jewels are blue, and that's the color of the chalk marks."

Ed shrugs and hauls open the heavy manhole cover. It's very dark down there. All you can see is the top of a steel ladder. Ed clambers down and disappears.

Zeke gulps. "Well, here goes nothing!" He follows Ed into the hole.

You take a deep breath and climb down after them.

It's almost pitch-dark when you reach the bottom of the ladder. You don't hear or see anything.

"Zeke!" you shout. "Ed!" Your voice echoes in the darkness.

You think you hear Ed calling from up ahead. You take a step toward the sound.

Then Zeke yells your name from the other direction.

Uh-oh. Which way do you go?

If you follow Ed, go to PAGE 62.
If you follow Zeke, go to PAGE 66.

"We'll never outswim them!" you yell. "They're *fish!*"

Your brain races as you try to think of a way to scare the fish. You just need enough time to make it to the other side of the pool.

"A cat!" you shout. "Fish are scared of cats, aren't they?"

"Who knows?" Zeke answers as he thrashes around in the water. "But let's try acting like cats."

Both of you start meowing as loudly as you can. "Meow! Meow!"

It doesn't sound very convincing to you, but it seems to confuse the fish. They turn and swim away, disappearing in the murky water.

"Those are really dumb fish," you comment. "Everyone knows cats don't swim."

"Let's go," Zeke responds. "Before they figure it out."

The two of you swim as hard as you can. Soon you feel the welcome hardness of the ledge on the other side of the pool. With a sigh of relief, you haul yourself out of the water.

You are plunged into darkness as the water immediately stops glowing.

Grope to PAGE 133.

"It will take too long to reach that log," you say. "Let's wade. It's only water."

You walk steadily into the muddy stream. Soon you're waist deep in the murky water. Your feet sink into the soft, mushy bottom. Something scaly brushes by your leg.

Reluctantly, Zeke follows you.

"This is disgusting!" he cries.

You don't say anything, but you think it's pretty disgusting too. You clamber out on the other side, dripping ooze and mud.

"You know, Zeke," you comment, "I hate to admit it, but you were right — we should have used the log."

As you speak, the "log" rolls over and opens its mouth. Even from far away, you can clearly see the rows of sharp yellow teeth.

"That's no log," Zeke whispers. "It's an alligator. A giant alligator!"

The gator starts swimming rapidly in your direction. You both watch, spellbound.

"Let's get out of here!" Zeke finally screams.

Run to PAGE 132.

"I didn't know," you apologize. "I'll stop it." You reach for the box.

Annabelle grabs your wrist. Her fingers feel like ice-cold steel on your skin.

"No!" she screams. "We must dance!"

"I don't know how to waltz!" you protest. But the ghost seizes your hands and whirls you across the ballroom. Your feet dangle above the dance floor.

"We will dance the way I should have danced that night," Annabelle cries. "We will dance forever!"

"Forever?" you repeat shakily.

"Forever!" she declares with a wild laugh. Then she begins to count the steps in time to the music.

"*One* two three, *one* two three . . ."

Well, Twinkle-Toes. Hope you have on your dancing shoes. Because when a *ghost* says forever, that's a very, very, very long time.

Have a ball!

THE END

118

You slip the cylinder labeled COME-BACK TANGO into the music box and wind the crank. Tinkly, sweet tones fill the air.

Annabelle floats toward you. "That was our favorite song," she says wistfully. "Mine and Hubert's. If only I hadn't been so jealous. Oh, I wish Hubert were here so I could see him one more time."

"I *am* here," a young man's voice calls.

You whirl around.

In the dark corner of the ballroom, a glowing light forms itself into a young man!

"Hubert!" Annabelle cries.

"Annabelle!" Hubert cries.

"Barf!" Zeke groans.

Annabelle's face glows with a rich pink light. She flies to the ghost of Hubert, her long-lost boyfriend. They hug.

Zeke nudges you. "I feel like I'm watching a sappy romance movie."

Hubert turns to you and clears his throat.

Listen to him on PAGE 122.

"The *Annabelle*," you blurt out. "Can you show us where she sank?"

Carl starts pacing in front of the hut. "Listened not, did you? There is no way! What Carl knows, he *never* shows!"

Carl is bugged out! you think. You glance around the clearing, looking for the path back to the lake.

You see a break in the underbrush. You aren't sure if it's the same path. But at least it leads *away* from Carl!

"Follow me," you tell Zeke. "I see a path. Let's follow it and see if it leads home — or to the *Annabelle*."

Zeke nods. You both wave good-bye to Carl and walk into the swamp. Soon you come to the bank of a wide, muddy stream.

"Come on," you tell Zeke. "Let's wade across."

"Who wants to get wet again?" Zeke replies. "There's a log up there that goes almost across. Let's walk on that."

The log bridge is a long way up the river. You figure it will take a while to hack through the brush to reach it.

But wading across the stream could be more dangerous than it looks. There could be poisonous snakes in the water. Or alligators!

What do you do?

Use the log bridge on PAGE 64.
Wade across on PAGE 116.

"Awesome!" Zeke cries. Then he peers at you. "Uh — how?"

"With this!" you reply, waving the book. "Annabelle's diary. I bet she knew how to get into the smugglers' tunnel."

"Hey! Maybe Annabelle even found the treasure," Zeke declares excitedly. "Maybe she wrote about that too."

You flip over the page you were reading.

Perfect!

"Look," you exclaim. "There's a map on the back of this page."

You show Zeke the other side of the yellowing paper.

"That's not a map," Zeke complains after looking at it. "It's a puzzle. See? It shows two secret doors in the wall over there. But only one door leads to the tunnel. To find the right door, we have to solve the puzzle."

You read the instructions on the puzzle. "It says here that the floor stones in the basement form a pattern," you tell Zeke.

Quickly, you and Zeke push aside old boxes until you can see most of the floor. There it is — a pattern in the stones. But what does it mean?

Puzzle it out on PAGE 39.

"Okay, what do I have to do?" you ask, trying to sound brave.

"Come with me," the ghost replies.

He floats into the large room that was once the riverboat's casino. Roulette wheels and blackjack tables lie on their sides. Playing cards and chips are scattered on the floor. You follow Zeke to a playing table covered with mold. He steps behind it and slaps on a tattered green visor. The hat looks eerie over his transparent face and bottomless black eyes.

He picks up a dusty old deck of playing cards. He shuffles them expertly, making them fly from hand to hand.

"We'll play a little game of chance," he explains. "All you have to do is pick the ace of spades. Find it and I'll set you free. I'll even give you the treasure. Choose the wrong card — and you will take my place here. Is it a deal?"

You swallow nervously. It's not a *good* deal. But what other choice do you have?

You nod silently.

Take a chance on PAGE 99.

"After that terrible night, I died of a broken heart," Hubert tells you. "I haunted this room, waiting for someone to break the curse so I could be with Annabelle again."

Annabelle faces you and Zeke. "Playing that song broke the spell. Now I will keep my part of the bargain. The treasure."

She waves her hand. A panel in the wall opens, revealing a large chest. The lid springs open. It is full of gold coins and bright jewels.

"Fill your pockets," Annabelle instructs. "Then Hubert and I will lead you home."

There's so much treasure in the trunk, you and Zeke barely make a dent as you stuff your pockets with gems.

"Now we will all leave the tunnels — forever," Annabelle declares.

"Forever!" Hubert cheers.

"Forever!" Zeke repeats.

They all turn and stare at you.

"Forever," you mumble, crossing your fingers behind your back. No way you're going to let all that treasure go to waste in a dark old tunnel. You'll be back. But for now it looks like your adventure has come to an

END.

Carl clears his throat and begins to recite:

"I've got three sticks on my head.
I've got four furs on my bed.
Add those numbers. Then take away one. That's the number of hides on my feet.
Three less than that is the number of meals I eat.
To get the number of my pet birds just add one,
Multiply my birds by three and you're almost done.
Subtract from that the number nine.
Now multiply by two and you're doing fine.
Now look at my head, and find the number of sticks.
To get the number of rungs, to the sticks add six."

You concentrate as the strange old man recites his riddle. You're trying to do the math in your head.

Before you can say anything, Zeke gives a triumphant cry.

"I've got it!" he shouts. "The answer is twelve!"

If you think Zeke is right, go to PAGE 134.
If you got a different answer, go to PAGE 98.

You jump from stone to stone, with Zeke right behind you. When you reach the wall you find yourself in the corner of the basement.

"No door," you grumble.

"It's a *hidden* door," Zeke points out. "Try pushing the wall."

Carefully you push against the wall. Nothing happens.

"We made a mistake!" you exclaim, and stamp your foot on the stone floor.

The wall falls away!

It's a trapdoor!

You drop forward into darkness. Zeke, who was leaning against you, loses his balance and falls with you.

"Help!" you scream.

But there's no one to hear you.

Fall to PAGE 26.

"Treasure!" Zeke shouts happily. "That's the *least* I can do for you."

Before long, you are walking slowly on the path back to Swamp House, with Zeke leading the way. You're walking slowly because you're burdened down with two sacks of gold that Zeke gave you as a reward.

"I guess I won't be seeing you around Swamp House anymore," you say with a touch of sadness.

"No, you won't," Zeke answers. He looks a little sad too, but he's already looking into the distance.

"It's time for me to be moving on," Zeke tells you. "I guess you'll be going back to your old neighborhood soon," he adds.

"I don't know about that," you tell him, grinning. "I'm starting to like it around here. It's a lot more interesting than my old neighborhood. Besides, Swamp House might be a nice place to live, with some fixing up. And a couple of bags of gold can do a lot of fixing up!"

THE END

Silently, you pull the notebook out of Billings's pack. Holding it up to the flickering firelight, you thumb through the pages.

The first entries are just boring notes about soil samples and trail markings.

Then you read something that makes you catch your breath:

"My plan to pretend I'm a park ranger has worked perfectly so far! No one suspects that I'm in this swamp to find that hag Annabelle and her magical potion. When I do, I will have powers that make me strong, rich, and immortal!"

Hurriedly you flip the pages, your heart beating faster. According to the notebook, Annabelle is supposed to be a witch! Her treasure is some kind of magic drink. And the way to find Annabelle is with a magic brass telescope!

You come to the last entry. Your hands shake as you read it.

"These stupid kids have somehow found the telescope," it says. "I've got to get it away from them. And then get rid of the little brats so no one else learns about Annabelle."

Scared and trembling, you realize what you have to do.

You have to run away!

Run to PAGE 48.

You and Zeke slowly approach Annabelle's hut.

"I know why you are here," she says. "You want the magical potion that promises wealth, and health, and power."

"That would be so awe —" Zeke begins, but you elbow him in the ribs.

"We don't need anything, ma'am," you state politely. "Except directions to get out of here."

You've decided that you don't want to drink anything this old woman is doling out!

"I'll be glad to sit down with you in the hut and draw you a map," Annabelle says. "But before you enter, you must drink from the cup of welcome."

She walks to a low bench near the doorway and points to three identical wooden cups.

"No thanks. I'm not thirsty," you answer.

"Choose one and drink!" Annabelle snaps. One of her dogs growls and steps toward you.

"Are these magic?" you ask.

"You'll find out soon enough," she warns. "Now, choose one and drink."

Drink from the cup on the right on PAGE 44.
Drink from the cup in the center on PAGE 130.
Drink from the cup on the left on PAGE 69.

You reach out and grab the red jewel.

"Wronnnng!"

Annabelle's triumphant shriek rings through the air.

"Fools!" she snarls. Her ghostly arms reach out, stretching like a white fog. You are rooted to the spot, trapped by some unseen power. Zeke trembles in terror beside you.

"Help!" he croaks feebly.

But there's no one to hear you. No one to help.

The fog fills your vision. Annabelle's ghostly form surrounds you. First you feel icy cold. Then you feel your solid body melting away. You hear Annabelle's laughter.

"Now you will be spirits like me," she cries. "Trapped in these tunnels for all eternity!"

It's tough luck, being turned into a ghost. But try to get into the *spirit* of things. Besides, you didn't really solve that puzzle, anyway.

You never had a ghost of a chance!

THE END

You take the book out of the cabin so you can read it by moonlight. You scan the pages. As you do, Zeke lays a ghostly hand on your arm. You can see right through it, to your sleeve.

"Don't look now," he whispers. "But we have company — again."

You glance up. Uh-oh. The ghost crew has come back!

Your hands shake so hard, you almost drop the logbook. Getting used to Zeke as a ghost is hard enough. The sight of dozens of them drifting toward you is a lot worse.

You suddenly remember the telescope. It scared them before! You pull it out and start to aim it at them. The ghosts wiggle backwards, but they don't go far.

Then you have a brilliant idea. You put the scope to your eye and peer at the logbook!

Just as you hoped, glowing letters light up on a page that appeared blank before.

You look up in triumph.

"Stop!" you command the ghosts. "This boy, Ezekiel, didn't sink your boat! And I can prove it!"

Show them on PAGE 46.

You lift the center cup to your mouth. What if it's poison? you think. Your hand is shaking so hard, you spill a few drops.

You nervously sip the liquid.

Not bad, you think. It tastes a little like apple juice. And that's supposed to be good for you.

You hand the cup to Zeke, and he drinks too.

"Hey!" you shout angrily. "Don't drink it all!"

Without thinking, you grab for the cup. The tasty liquid spills on the ground.

"You spilled it!" Zeke yells. Then he bursts into tears!

You stare at Zeke. He's wailing at the top of his lungs.

"Oh, don't be such a baby!" you try to say, except it comes out, "Oh doo bee soo gee baba!"

What's happening?

Turn to PAGE 88.

"I don't dare pick the jewel up," you think.

In the next second Annabelle's unseen power has drawn you forward. The jewel-like object is beyond reach.

You and Zeke are pulled through the near-darkness. It seems as if hours go by. Finally Annabelle stops. Right in front of the door to your basement! It's smooth and solid, with a hole where the doorknob should be.

"To lift the curse, I must return home!" she cries. "Open the door."

Freed from her spell, you and Zeke throw yourselves at the door. You pull and tug, but it doesn't budge. Finally, you give up and slump against the door, exhausted.

"You've failed!" Annabelle cries. "I will never return home! But neither shall you!"

From out of nowhere a powerful wind roars against you. The ground shakes, and rocks fall from the ceiling.

"The cavern is collapsing!" Zeke shouts.

Heavy boulders drop on all sides. You look up and see a chunk of granite the size of a car falling straight toward you.

You're scared stiff. But look on the bright side. Now you don't have to go to school tomorrow!

THE END

132

You and Zeke dash onto the path. On one side, the river flows by. On the other side is a dense wall of vegetation. As you trot along, you glance at the water. The gator is swimming along next to the path, watching you with its cold yellow eyes.

"Let's step on it, Zeke," you urge. "That gator looks hungry!"

You speed up, squinting to see as the sun begins to sink. The stream gets wider and wider. Finally it joins a broad, slow-moving river covered with brown scum and trailing vines.

The alligator is still swimming next to the path — and it's closer to the shore now! You get the feeling that it's just waiting to make its move. Maybe it's waiting for the sun to go down!

Trot faster to PAGE 63.

You and Zeke stand up, dripping water on the cold stone floor.

"The flashlight!" you cry. "I must have left it on the other side of the pool."

For a moment you panic. Then you see a light coming from the tunnel in front of you. Awesome! you think. It must be a way out!

You and Zeke rush toward the light.

You run through the tunnel. The walls close in. And you can tell by the steep slope that you are heading deeper and deeper.

Maybe it's not the way out, you think. But it's the only way to go. The light grows brighter.

Then you stop dead. The hair on the back of your neck goes up. Because you can see where the light is coming from.

And you've never felt this scared in your life.

"Wh-wh-what *is* that?" Zeke whispers.

Turn to PAGE 9.

"Th-that sounds right," you stammer, even though you don't feel sure at all. "Twelve rungs!"

Carl stares down at you for a moment. Then he cackles with glee.

"Thought it was easy, did you?" he cries. "But you can't catch Carl! Wrong you are! Trapped with my friends you are!"

Carl disappears, and you hear his cackling fade away.

"What a freak," Zeke comments. "But what did he mean by his 'friends'? We're alone down here."

"Yeah. I don't see anyone," you agree. You feel relieved. If Carl's friends are anything like him, you'll pass!

Then you hear a faint scratching sound. It gets louder. And louder.

"What's that?" Zeke cries.

"I don't know," you answer, your heart pounding. "But I think Carl's friends just got here."

Meet them on PAGE 40.

About R.L. Stine

R.L. Stine is the most popular author in America. He is the creator of the *Goosebumps, Give Yourself Goosebumps, Fear Street,* and *Ghosts of Fear Street* series, among other popular books. He has written more than 100 scary novels for kids. Bob lives in New York City with his wife, Jane, teenage son, Matt, and dog, Nadine.

Shop Till You Drop... Dead!

GIVE YOURSELF

Goosebumps®

R.L. STINE

Reader Beware—You Choose the Scare.
You're about to spend the midnight
hour inside a department store called
Mayfield's Bazaar—seven floors of terror! The bizarrest bazaar in town is
home to a mannequin that comes to
life, a very unsafe elevator, and creatures who only come out at night, like
the giant acid-sliming slug. It's an after-
hours fright fest, whichever floor you
choose…

#25 SHOP TILL YOU DROP...DEAD

GIVE YOURSELF Goosebumps®

...WITH 20 DIFFERENT SCARY ENDINGS IN EACH BOOK!

R.L. STINE

$3.99 EACH

Scare me, thrill me, mail me GOOSEBUMPS now!

SCHOLASTIC

PARACHUTE

IT'S COMING FOR YOU.

Get Ready To Be Scared